THE
BLACK
CAROUSEL

THE
BLACK
CAROUSEL

CHARLES GRANT

TOR

A TOM DOHERTY ASSOCIATES BOOK
NEW YORK

THE BLACK CAROUSEL

Copyright © 1995 by Charles Grant

This book is printed on acid-free paper.

A Tor Book
Published by Tom Doherty Associates, Inc.
175 Fifth Avenue
New York, N.Y. 10010

Tor ® is a registered trademark of Tom Doherty Associates, Inc.

Design by Lynn Newmark

Library of Congress Cataloging-in-Publication Data
Grant, Charles L.
    The black carousel / Charles Grant.
        p.   cm.
    "A Tom Doherty Associates book."
    ISBN 0–312–85791–8
    I. Title.
    PS3557.R265B57   1995
    813'.54—dc20   94–36022
                                                             CIP

First edition: January 1995

Printed in the United States of America

0 9 8 7 6 5 4 3 2 1

For Ashley, the Badger Queen,
Who knows that a carousel's not just for kids;
With four rides, some Bailey's,
And not the least, affection.

PROLOGUE

S TARS FALL IN SUMMER, AND IT MAKES NO DIFFERENCE when someone claims that the light in the night sky isn't really a star. Stars fall, just like gods, and like fallen gods there's no sense searching for the site of their graves. There are no craters, no ashes, no explosions that at least give the dying a brilliant moment of satisfaction. A flare. A glance. A pointing finger to mark the trail.

Nothing more.

Nothing after.

People are the same.

Not the geniuses, the truly special, who put the lie to the notion that we're all created equal; it's the other one—

the one who sits alone on the porch after supper and listens to the neighborhood wind itself down toward sunset, drink or newspaper in one hand, the other on the armrest, holding on;

the one who walks the dog and changes the litter box and tunes the car engine and vacuums the carpets and scolds the baby and suddenly stands in the middle of the staircase, mo-

mentarily confused, one hand lightly touching a throat, the
other on the banister, holding on;

the one who can't figure out where the hell it all went because it was only yesterday—and it had to have been only yesterday, for crying out loud—that he had all his hair and she
had no laugh lines and he could sprint a block without losing
his breath and she could fit into the dress she wore the night
she graduated from college . . . and they stand in the middle of
the kitchen, staring at strangers, perplexed, bewildered, not
wanting to cry because there is no tangible hurt, not wanting
to scream because the monsters aren't real, but afraid to move
or speak because they're too busy, holding on.

It has nothing to do with attaching a meaning to a life; it
has everything to do with measuring the length of that flare
that barely lights up the night sky.

It has everything to do with holding on.

At that point, Callum Davidson shook his head and walked
away, to fetch, he said over his shoulder, either drinks or ra-
tions of poison for the rest of us, and Nina Hunt said, "Gee,
and I thought shooting stars were supposed to be romantic.
Silly me."

We were, that night, escapees from the boisterous recep-
tion going on in my house. A lot of townspeople, a lot of laughter and chatter and nudging and sideways glances; food
catered by Gale Winston from the Cock's Crow, drinks thanks
to Nigel Oxley at the Brass Ring. I provided the space because
they asked me, and because I couldn't think of one damn reason why not.

Nina, four-year proprietor of Melody Tapes and Records,
had lugged over a carton of records and compact discs that everyone picked over and no one listened to while they were

playing. And when I suggested some fresh air, she grabbed my arm, grabbed Callum's, and we lit out for the territory—in this case, the patch of green and trees and nightdark flowers in front of my house.

"What's the problem?" she asked after a while of staring at the houses across the street, at the empty street itself, and at the evergreen shrubs that lined the base of the porch. "You lose a bet?"

I smiled, albeit wanly. Until that moment, I had no idea why I'd been smothered in such gloom. After all, the Station was welcoming its new chief of police; the reconstruction of Centre Street, after a number of political and economic delays, was at last completed and most of the shop and office facades finally remodeled to everyone's satisfaction; and all was supposedly right with the world.

"Don't know," I said, leaning back against a bole.

"A writer's thing, huh?"

I frowned.

"Moods," she explained, as if I should have known. A tiny creature without seeming short, hair woven from ebony, skin that took the sun without looking like leather. "Up, down, sometimes sideways, for no reason at all. All great poets are reputed to be temperamental, you know."

"I'm not a poet."

"No kidding."

Wan smile, instant grin.

A waft of laughter from the backyard, where lights had been strung and tables set out. I looked that way, massaged the back of my neck.

Callum returned and handed each of us a glass. When Nina questioned him with a tilt of her head, he stood tall—

which was very tall indeed—and glared indignantly. "Madam, if I were going to poison you, I wouldn't ruin perfectly good Scotch doing it."

She chuckled.

Callum drank and said, "So?"

I bridled a little. "What the hell's going on? You guys think I'm going to cut my throat or something?"

He took a spot beside me, shoulder against the bark. "No, but I think that you think you've already run the race, my friend. You never reached the top, the way's too crowded now with people who have more energy, the only way left is down. And if I know you, and I do, you're about to go into a funk that'll keep you from working for weeks."

"Go to hell."

He grinned at Nina. "See?"

He was wrong, and he was so right I wanted to throttle him, but, as I proceeded to tell him without meeting his gaze, my immediate concern was the new top cop. Not a big man was Deric Stockton, but he was large enough to be intimidating if he had to be. He also had the laconic manner all Stocktons seem to have had, and no fear at all that he was about to take over a job that had been held by his family with few exceptions since Lucas Stockton inaugurated the position, back in the middle of the nineteenth century.

What I didn't know, what none of us knew, was how much he understood about Oxrun Station.

And when he found out, how long it would be before he was on the next train out—the direction wouldn't matter.

Nina said nothing. Though she hadn't lived here very long, she had picked up on things almost at once, had come to terms with them, and accepted them.

Callum knew far more, and though he often fought—with

me, with himself, with anyone who would listen—he hadn't
run either. He couldn't. Those of us who loved movies new
and old wouldn't let him. He ran the Regency Theater, on
Centre Street, elegant home for all our fantasies, the raft we
sometimes used to get away from the terrors that lurked
around us on the shore.

"I think," he said a few minutes later, "he'll be all right. He
was Abe's kid brother, after all, and Abe must have told him
something."

"I guess."

Nina looked at the house. "And if he didn't, you will."

"What?"

I saw it then, the look between them, and I felt like a complete jerk for not catching on the minute I had been asked to
open my house tonight. Of course.

"You're kidding," I said.

Deric Stockton came to the door, came out, and saw us.

"Who better?" Callum wanted to know.

"Nat Clayton," I answered instantly. "Librarians know everything; Nat knows even more. Or Marc—newspaper editors
are notoriously nosy and gabby. And being Nat's husband, he's
worse than most." I held up a hand, touched a finger. "Cyd
Yarrow's back in town—god knows she could tell him a thing
or two. You want more? No problem. What about old Fred
Borg, retired but not forgotten, from that selfsame police
force? Not to mention a couple of teachers I could—"

"All right, all right," Callum said sourly. "Jesus, you're
touchy."

"Moody," Nina corrected.

I almost laughed.

Stockton came down the steps, clearly uncomfortable in
his dark blue suit, his still-fair hair slicked back but making a

determined effort to cut loose, like his handlebar mustache. Although the light behind him put his face in shadow, it was evident he was Abe's brother—every line carved deep, every angle sharp and ridged, eyes deep set and much too old for the man who used them.

"Evening," he said.

We nodded, listened to the crickets, listened to the music, listened to the way time slowed on summer evenings. Comfortable. A few words about the season, the entertainments at the college, bits of gossip Davidson doled out without having to be told, or scolded about, a shifting of positions until Nina was with me at the tree, and the two men faced us, glancing up at the night birds fussing in the leaves.

"I'm going to like it here," Deric allowed into a silence that cut us off from the Station. He nodded, scratched the side of his nose. "Figure I'll get along."

A round of nods and grunts and shifting of feet.

He looked straight at me then. "I'm told you can help me."

I didn't answer.

Nina poked me, the disapproving kind that made me feel like a kid who'd forgotten to say thank you.

"Abe wrote, you know."

I could hear it then—*you loved that old man and so did I, he said I should listen . . . so I'm listening.*

Right.

Some kids rode past on their bicycles, balloons tied to the handlebars, playing cards snapping against the spokes. A party somewhere, something doing at the grade school or at a church; a few seconds later another group sped by, faster, louder, voices echoing off the houses and swallowed by the dark. I put my hands in my pockets and walked down to the sidewalk, watching the reflectors catch the streetlamps until they were little more than red sparks that winked out when a breeze came at me from around the corner.

Sparks.

Flares.

I turned around.

"You ever hear of Pilgrim's Travelers?"

Callum cleared his throat noisily. "I'm not sure—"

"Well?" I asked, pointedly ignoring him.

Deric shook his head, slowly. "Don't think so."

Nina said, "Me neither."

Callum questioned me without saying a word, and when I nodded, he offered to refresh all our drinks. We accepted, and he made me promise not to begin until he returned. An easy promise, because if Deric wanted to know about the Station, wanted to hear it from a source besides a brother's letter, I was going to need fortification.

Not in the liquor.

The company.

I looked up at the stars I could see above the house, thought of those kids and their bikes and how they had reminded me of parties, and how the parties had reminded me of carnivals and fairs. Flares themselves, but blinding for a night or a weekend and just as swiftly gone, leaving behind nothing but an empty field, a blowing wind, tracks in the earth, and the smell not of cotton candy and candied apples, not of greasepaint and grease, but of a slow smiling dying.

The way a carousel sounds when the last tune's been played and the animals stop spinning.

I led Nina and Deric to the steps, and we sat, took our glasses when Callum joined us, and I plucked with some trouble an ice cube from my drink.

"Imagine," I said, "what it must be like when all the ice

melts and there's nothing left to hold but the cold air left behind."

"Hey," Nina said softly, and placed a light hand on my knee.

This time I did smile.

"It's okay," I told her. "I'm not the one who's dying. Tonight." She squeezed; I covered her fingers. I looked to Deric and said, "Abe ever tell you about a guy called Casey? A carpenter named Kayman? People like that?"

He shook his head. "Are they . . . what did you call them, Pilgrim's Travelers?"

"No," I answered, dropping what was left of the ice cube back into the glass. "No, but they were there. Holding on."

I

Penny Tunes for a
Gold Lion

A WAGON'S BROAD PAINTED WHEELS RATTLED AND slipped over the cobblestones that night, its team of old black geldings snorting in their traces, the driver's voice carrying through the early morning fog, urging the horses on in a practiced monotone.

The sound of a lazy whip.

The rattling of a harness.

Hooves clattering on stone, striking sparks, moving on.

Another wagon, much heavier, a caravan that carried with it the tuneless, oddly melodic jangle of a dozen tin bells hanging from a brace above the locked doors in back.

A third to make it a procession, and the soft quiet sound of a young woman laughing.

"There's nothing to it," said Casey Bethune from his customary place at the door end of the bar. "The damn things are weighted."

"So if there's nothing to it, what's the trick?"

Casey looked in wonder at the other men and women on

the stools down toward the other end and not paying attention, looked in comic disbelief at the big man seated at his left hand, immediately around the bar's squared corner. "The trick? That's easy—you don't even try."

Mayard Chase stared.

"Think," Casey urged gently and with a smile.

Chase wrinkled his face, put a finger to his temple, closed his eyes.

From behind the bar Molly Burgess stopped washing glasses and looked at Casey. "What's Yard doing?"

"Thinking."

"Quiet," Chase demanded. "I'm thinking."

"Drunk," Molly said with a knowing nod.

"Thinking," Casey insisted. "I've told him a kind of joke and he still doesn't get it."

"Oh God save us," she said. "We'll be here all night."

"Hush," Chase commanded, opened one eye, closed it again. "There's got to be a trick to the trick, you see. Casey wouldn't know straight if he was whacked with a ruler."

Molly groaned and walked away; Casey grinned after her and took a careful sip of his drink, a small Scotch and soda, only his second that night and probably his last. He was going to Pilgrim's Travelers later on, and he wanted his head clear, his eye keen, his arm steady. He was going to win a stuffed panda if it killed him.

Another sip, and he looked around him, not seeing much because all of it was as familiar as the lumps in his mattress.

The Brass Ring was long and narrow, bar on the right and small round tables on the left; the aisle between, bare hardwood and comfortably scuffed; beyond, more tables in two rows, and beyond them an open space for those who attacked the three dartboards each night, making more noise than an army in full rout. Gleaming brass horse braces on the grey-wood walls, brass rail top and bottom around the bar, electric lanterns anchored on thick shelves just wide enough to hold them kept twilight inside no matter where the sun was. The only window faced Centre Street, and its lower half was veiled by a burgundy curtain hung from brass rings on a brass rod; the outside wall, along Steuben, had been painted by the owner to resemble three arched, frosted windows so realistically done that more than one evening pedestrian had paused to peer through the painted panes and abruptly walked away as if nothing had happened.

No food was served here, just pretzels and salted peanuts. Casey loved it.

The Mariner Lounge and the Chancellor Inn made him uncomfortable; the Cock's Crow, while more his style, was sometimes just too far away, and too often too crowded. The Brass Ring, then, was a godsend. It had opened three months ago on the same site as its namesake, which had shut its doors in 1897 after less than five years' operation. This one, he thought as he waited for Yard, was bound to last much longer. The atmosphere was amiable without forcing anyone to be friendly when they weren't in the mood, the liquor and beer inexpensive, and Nigel Oxley, the owner and sometimes dart player, didn't insist on his customers drinking just as long as they bought something during their stay.

Yard relaxed with a sharp sigh. "I give up."

"You give up."

"That's what I said. I give up. What's the trick?"

Casey massaged the side of his neck, the backs of his hands. "Yard, pay attention, boy—the bottles are weighted, you see—only a Goliath could knock them over with the spongy softballs they give you, so . . . you . . ." He waited expectantly.

Chase nodded. Waiting.

"Jesus," Casey said. "Damnit, man, it's all rigged against you so you don't even try!"

"Ah."

"Right." He grabbed a handful of peanuts from a chipped wood bowl, dropped one into his mouth. "Yard, how the hell do you make a living with that store, huh? Seems to me you'd get robbed blind in three days."

"Two," said Yard. "But I'm independently wealthy."

Grinning, Casey shook his head, looked down at his glass, at the polished wood. His face was there in dark reflection, but he couldn't see it clearly. Lean and leathered like the rest of him, eyes in a constant partial squint, lips in a perpetual lopsided smile, topped by a mass of combed-back hair that had begun to turn white while he was still in high school, finished its turning before he'd graduated from college. A number of dyes and colorings had been tried before he gave up—they only made him look foolish, unnatural, made him look like a stranger had claimed squatter's rights in his bathroom mirror.

Mayard Chase, on the other hand, was high and wide, with a carpenter's hands and a bricklayer's muscles, and virtually no hair at all above a face round and fleshy. The owner of the hardware store had tried, only once, a toupee. Two summers ago, to keep his pate from burning and peeling. Neither his children nor his wife had had the nerve to tell him what he looked like; not so his friends. The rug was gone in a week.

A cry of victory from a dart game, applause and a call for a round of drinks on the losers for those at the back tables.

The door opened to admit three men and a woman; they hesitated for a moment, listened to the noise, and left.

Your loss, he thought, sipped, looked around again, and nodded to the two women seated at the first table by the door.

Both wore their hair short and brushed back over their ears, both wore T-shirts and jeans and tennis shoes without socks. The older was near his age, a teacher at the high school; the other was a decade less, though her sharp-angled face erased the difference until she smiled. Ordinarily he wouldn't speak to them other than a polite greeting, a polite farewell; tonight, however, Yard's feigned obtuseness had put him in good humor.

"You ladies going to the fair?" he asked, though he was careful to make it clear the question was no invitation.

The teacher shook her head. "Not tonight. Summer school tomorrow. Probably Friday, if I bother."

Her companion didn't answer.

Yard swiveled around on his stool, leaned back on one elbow, paunch separating the buttons of his checkered shirt. "Better watch it there, Tina. Casey's on vacation these days, and when he's not making love to his damn flowers, he's hunting for human action."

Tina Elby raised a thick eyebrow. "Casey?"

Casey's smile felt strained, and he looked back to his glass. He wasn't in the mood for any of Yard's teasing, but it was his own fault for opening his big mouth in the first place.

"It's his job, you see," Yard continued, deepening his voice. "He sees all you beautiful women on his rounds every morning, he saves it all up for his free days."

"Yard," he said quietly, "knock it off."

Chase ignored him. "You don't know him the way I do. We all know him as a superior postman, a gardener without peer, a man who paints his whole house every time it gets a spot of mud. But beneath that innocent white hair lies the cunning brain of a lustful, debauched, and I might say extraordinarily experienced, man of the world."

"Yard."

A sideways glance at the table caught Tina grinning, and at the same time the grin told him she knew what Yard was doing. It should have made him feel better. It didn't. It only stirred a blush somewhere beneath his chin, a blush that would eventually darken his cheeks and made his hair seem all the lighter if his friend didn't soon shut his mouth.

"Prick," the other woman said flatly.

Yard blinked.

Tina frowned. "Norma, he's only kidding, for Pete's sake. Casey doesn't mind, do you, Case?"

Caught between a gape and a laugh, he managed a quick nod, then a shake of his head, then a "No, I don't care, let him talk, I'll tell his wife."

"Screw it, he's still a prick," Norma Hobbs muttered darkly, shoving her empty glass stein against the wall to join several others. She turned her head. "And that one's a creep. A so-called man who talks to stupid goddamn flowers. Nothing but goddamn weeds, plow 'em the hell under."

"Oh Jesus." Tina's expression was at once apologetic and helpless, but Yard had already turned his back, and all Casey could do was smile and shrug and turn away himself.

He came in twice a week, usually Wednesday and Friday, nursed two drinks and left. Sometimes Tina was here, most of the time she wasn't, and it suited him during her absence to develop conversations that would lead them from the bar to a table, and eventually to dinner. He had no illusions. She was attractive; he was plain. She was gone most of every summer, traveling around the country, seeing the world on package deals and her savings; he didn't like flying, and spent his free time in his garden. She was friendly, but had never hinted; he was courteous, and didn't know what to do next.

For him the situation was perfect.

Suddenly Norma lurched to her feet and swayed against the table. "Gotta go home," she announced angrily. "Son of a bitch, gotta go home."

Tina was up just as fast, and with a mouthed *sorry about this, guys,* followed her friend out the door.

Another cheer from the back.

Molly asked them loudly to keep it down, she was going deaf.

"You know," Yard said without turning his head, "if you try real hard, you might get to know her better in a hundred years or so."

"Who, Molly?"

"The teacher, stupid."

Casey cupped his glass between his palms. "I like Norma better. She hates men."

"Nope. Only her husband, because he left her."

"Jesus, Yard, he didn't leave her, for Christ's sake. He had cancer. He died. Jesus."

Chase shrugged and shook his head; it was all the same to him—he wasn't concerned with the bitch, only the teacher.

Casey checked his watch, then, and emptied his glass. "Time to go." He slid off the stool.

"Already?" Chase scowled at his own timepiece. "Maybe one more."

"Suit yourself. But it's almost the last night, and I'm not going to miss it."

He dropped a bill on the bar, waved good-bye to Molly, and headed for the door. It didn't matter if Yard joined him or not. Sooner or later they'd separate anyway, and he'd be alone. Which was just how he liked it.

At the entrance he paused and checked back over his shoulder.

Yard waved him on expansively. "Catch up to you later, maybe. The kids are supposed to meet me anyway. Down at the corner, not here," he added quickly.

"Right," Casey said.

Right, he thought, and hurried outside before Chase changed his mind.

As the door hissed shut behind him, he hesitated before turning right, but the women were gone, and that was fine, just fine. Hands slipped into his pockets, shoulders rolled, first one, then the other.

The sky was still light at just past eight o'clock, but Centre Street was dark in the building shadows that had already reached the other side. No pedestrians now, no traffic since the street had been repaved in brick, the sound of his footsteps muffled in the heat that settled on his back, a damp weight that made his throat paradoxically dry and his lungs labor. Neon too bright. Windows too dark. The trees at the curbs chattering with birds settling in until dawn.

Day above, night below.

The contrast made him uneasy. As if the Station, when evening crawled down from the surrounding wooded hills, slipped out of the real world and into a vast cavern where lights made monsters of simple rocks and boulders, and shadows made people out of simple dust in the air. As a postman he knew all the shops and offices, and most of the homes, could find them by touch if he had to, even by scent here and there.

Except at night.

When it changed.

Well, he said to a brief image in a window, you're in a mood tonight, aren't you?

Day above.

Handing out, with the regular mail, slick color leaflets of Pilgrim's Travelers, photographs and cartoons that promised rides and food and thrills and laughs and wonders and bright lights. It was the first time the carnival had come to the Station since he'd moved here, almost a decade ago, and all those he had spoken to swore it was something he would never forget. Not just a small-time local carny, a poor excuse for a country fair, but a kept promise of great times. When asked where it came from, some waved vaguely south, others vaguely west. It didn't matter much, it was here again, and a place as isolated as Oxrun Station took its surprises without question.

Night below.

He didn't much like the circus, and after childhood had been buried, he discovered that he didn't much like fairs either. It was too easy to see the ragged patches in the tents, the bored eyes of the barkers, the faded paint, the rigged games, the weary animals, the prices too high and the food too greasy and the nicotine stains on the fingers of the dancers who were supposed to boil his blood. Something had gone missing. He had once supposed it was the unquestioning joy of the child no longer in him, but he knew that wasn't strictly true; he guessed a growing cynicism the older he became and reality became too real, but that wasn't it either.

Hell, he just didn't know.

And he didn't know, really, why he was going tonight, except that all the people on his route before his vacation began had spoken of nothing else, not even the miserable weather, the lack of rain. And since the Travelers was, after all, clearly a rare beast, he decided he owed it to them and their morning conversations to at least have a look.

Maybe he'd be lucky and see Norma get squashed by a rogue elephant or eaten by a gorilla.

He chuckled, chided himself for such an uncharitable thought, and chuckled again.

A right on Chancellor Avenue slapped the setting sun into his eyes. He shaded them with one hand and nearly tripped over the police station's wide bottom step. A curse, a glance around to be sure no one had seen him, and he walked on. Joined by the end of the block by a few others, families and couples, a handful of loners like himself, heading toward Mainland Road and all in high humor, though none seemed in a great hurry. They called to him, children danced up to and away from him, and it wasn't long before he felt himself smiling.

This, he decided, is a pretty good idea. A kind of kick in the ass to get him out of the doldrums he'd sunk into lately. Nothing he could put his finger on, nothing he could trace from a specific source—just a feeling that getting up in the morning was too much a chore, that going home to an empty house each night was too much like lowering himself into a well-tended grave. The Brass Ring had been a way to put off the latter.

Molly, all blond ringlets and huge brown eyes, told him last week it was his midlife crisis.

What crisis? he had answered with an explosive forced laugh; I'm thirty-seven, unmarried, no children, no promotion in sight, just enough money in the bank to keep me from starving. That's no crisis, that's a goddamn fact of life.

Poor baby, she had cooed, and kissed him on the cheek.

Poor baby, he had thought, and wanted to tear out her lovely throat.

* * *

A rake with a broken handle bound together by fraying twine drawn over the ground; weeds and small stones filled straw baskets that were carried to the field's edge and dumped into a pit; several men with ball peen hammers pounding stakes, raising tents, singing without words to a mouth organ's lead.

A corral enclosed by four thick strands of rope, the horses inside grazing, eating hay, running along the perimeter and kicking their heels; another corral, this one for pigs, a few sheep, a few goats—grazing, eating hay, gnawing at the ropes until a small boy with a whip-branch snapped a nose, snapped a brow.

A trained bear, a dying tiger, ponies that gave rides in the afternoon and were trick-ridden by a hooded dwarf when the sun went down; several young women, and one not so young, dancing on a stage that sagged in the middle, enticing the crowd, promising with veils and winks and colored gauze and soft moans, that inside, behind the flap, the devil waited with more; a caravan with a sign that marked a fortune-teller, others that suggested fair games of chance, still others whose sides had been lifted up and propped open, the sweet and sour and bitter aromas of foreign cooking drifting with steam.

A tall woman at the entrance in the garb of a Great White Hunter, pistol strapped to her side, greeting the families and the couples and the loners who came from the carriages and traps parked at the side of the road, from the automobiles and buses parked on the verge. She answered all questions with a joke, flirted with all the men and told all the women with a look that their men were safe here, thrust a hip at the boys and showed the girls how to do it.

Harps and harmonicas and violins and horns and a piano and a tambourine and a calliope and an organ.

And in the alleys between the tents and the concession

stands and the caravans and the trucks and the wagons, the soft quiet sound of a young woman laughing.

Casey crossed Mainland Road and angled to his left, toward one of four broad wood ramps that had been placed across the drainage ditch on the other side. A thorn hedge had been cut down here, and he climbed the slope on another ramp and stood to one side, hands on his hips, doubt his expression.

It was all ebony and silhouette because of the lowering sun.

Cutouts they were, unreal, that swallowed the people who walked under the high filigree wood arch, reaching up to a man on a high stool on either side who exchanged money for tickets, jokes for jokes, questions for directions.

It was huge.

There were lights strung on wire through the air, hanging from wire along the fence that marked the fair's boundary; from somewhere in the back was a spotlight that still hadn't the strength to quite match the light still lingering in the sky.

It amazed him.

What he had expected was something on the far side of tacky, something dusty and run-down and showing its age, something he could move through in an hour and still have time for another drink with Molly; what he saw as he moved forward and could see through the arch gate was enough to keep him busy for this night and ten others.

I'll be damned, he thought; I'll be damned.

The entrance fee was ten dollars, and the ticket man assured him that he wouldn't have to pay for anything else, unless he got hungry.

He nodded, clumsily pinned the ticket to his breast pocket as he'd been instructed, and stepped inside, onto a wide, bare earth midway lined with game booths and food stands so brightly painted, so individually done, that if someone had said *I'll meet you in an hour by the purple dragon*, he would have known exactly where to be.

Incredible.

He strolled on.

Unbelievable.

A short distance in was an intersection, the games and food continuing left and right; straight ahead, amusement tents and caravans—dancers, singers, a variety show, a sword swallower, a magician, much more.

He stood in the center and couldn't make up his mind, was angry that he couldn't because this wasn't supposed to be. He had been ready to starve, not be given a feast.

"Hey, Mr. Bethune!"

He spun around, then sidestepped deftly when a gang of kids charged past him. One, a young girl he recognized as being new to the Station, skidded to a halt and would have fallen if he hadn't grabbed her arm.

"Easy does it, Fran," he cautioned, grinning as she panted, and thumped at her chest. "You're going to kill yourself before the fireworks."

"Fireworks?" Eyes under dark hair widened in delight. "Really? Fireworks?" She looked around anxiously. "Where? Where will they be?"

He laughed. "Tell you the truth, I don't know if there'll even be any. I just got here myself." Her clear disappointment made him feel like a rat, and he tapped her shoulder lightly. "But look, this is a fair, right? So you have to have fireworks. I mean, what would a fair be without them?"

Peering after her friends, Fran shrugged. "I don't know. I've never seen one."

"You're kidding."

She shook her head, crossed her heart. "They don't have fairs in Cambridge, Mr. Bethune. Not like this, I mean."

He almost laughed again because he knew the girl wasn't happy with the move from her old home. Every morning, bringing the mail, he had the distinct feeling she was waiting for news that her father had somehow, miraculously, been fired and they'd have to return to the city. Where they didn't have fairs.

He knew how she felt.

As beautiful as it was with its old homes and older hills, the valley farms and shallow creeks, the Station did that to some people. As if it were alive and, walking home at night, it watched, it waited, like a dark patient beast in the mouth of a monstrous cave. Nothing threatening, nothing dangerous. Just watching. Waiting. For something to go wrong.

A shrill call above the music that had suddenly sprung up from a dozen, a hundred directions at once. Fran turned and waved wildly, looked up at him and said, "Elly says there's a real neat merry-go-round over there someplace. All kinds of animals and things. You wanna come?"

He was too surprised to answer immediately, and when the summons came a second time, she blurted something about meeting him there maybe and raced away, expertly dodging between the legs of grown-ups too tall to notice her, vanishing just as he regained his voice and said, "Sure."

Sure?

What the hell are you doing, Casey, making a date with a kid?

He didn't know; he didn't care; he found a stand that sold ice cream and had them make him a cone that nearly toppled from its height. He licked it, wiped ice cream from his nose, and followed without meaning to a group of teenagers too busy pushing and shoving one another to pay attention to the glares their boisterous behavior provoked. He glared at them himself, nearly threw his cone at them when they collided with an elderly couple barely able to move along. The old man said something, but the teens didn't stop, only laughed, pushed and shoved, and broke into a run.

As he passed the couple, Casey wanted to say something, but he couldn't think what and so left it alone.

Stopping at a tent whose face was painted with fire, taunting demons in the flames, avenging angels above, a man in clerical garb on a platform before it all, upraised Bible in one hand, growling torch in the other, promising miracles of the prophets for those who entered and believed;

stopping at a low square building with a painted skull surrounding the entrance, ghosts in flight, a banshee, an undersea creature, a man dressed like Frankenstein's monster telling all the men that this was the place to get the girls hopping into their laps, thrills and excitement, a money-back guarantee if you didn't first die of fright;

stopping at a tent painted in warm browns and tans and comforting gold, palm trees and a cactus and a beautiful woman in a long-fringed bikini dancing to a flute played by a young boy sitting cross-legged below her, the barker winking at the men, suggesting the women move on and give their guys a break from the old ball-and-chain, the women giggling, the men either blushing or posing, the flute never pausing, as if the dancer were a cobra that either swayed or struck;

stopping at a second intersection, under the corner rope of another tent, finishing his cone and wiping his hands on his jeans, the lights brighter, almost a glare that made him look up to see that the sky had gone dark, the sun gone, though the heat hadn't left.

Idly he watched the crowds move like schools of tropical fish. Dozens of them, then nothing, then dozens more and nothing again. Playing in the coral, no sharks to fear and sharks hiding all over. A pair of lovers kissing fervently while still walking, his hand burrowed in her hip pocket, her hand tucked in his waistband. A silently weeping child in a stroller, red-faced and barely able to stay awake. A clown blowing a balloon for a little boy in a sailor suit. A cowgirl showing a comically intent man how to twirl a lasso.

The music.

The aromas.

The voices.

The noise.

Adults and kids with someplace to go.

Suddenly Casey closed his eyes and felt like crying, didn't understand why . . . unless it was because they had someplace to go.

"Nonsense," he snapped at himself, cleared his throat, cleared it again, and not caring where he went followed the sound of an old song he thought he knew, focusing on it, humming it, turning a corner and seeing the fair open up into an oval of several acres that held at least a dozen rides, from tiny clanging fire engines on circular tracks to the Octopus, whose jointed steel arms lifted spinning cabs into the dark beyond the reach of the lights. Shrieks and wails and children pointing and parents grinning and at the back, barely seen, the pointed circus top of a carousel.

He stared at it, frowning, moving sideways around the oval's rim as if losing sight of it would vanish it before he could reach the place where a line had formed.

It was black. Gleaming, faceted, strung with hundreds of

red and orange bulbs, the glow beneath its canopy falling a mistlike green upon the animals and their riders, the mirrors in the center housing rimmed with glittering gold, tall rectangles that reflected a thousand worlds that lived in their faces for less than an instant. Halfway there, he spotted Fran on an ostrich, kicking her legs and leaning over, trying to grab the tail of a fleeing giant rabbit. A half turn of the base and he stopped, mouth agape, when Mayard Chase whirled past with a child in his lap, atop a kangaroo and pointing a stern finger at another child beside him, on a snarling hyena.

He hoped Yard hadn't had too much more to drink, or there'd be one hell of an embarrassed hardware man once the carousel stopped spinning.

A little closer, and he noticed a cleared area on the far side of the ride, off to his left. Well, I'll be damned, he thought. It was a dance floor twenty or thirty feet on a side, with at least a dozen couples happily waltzing to the music the carousel played. He recognized a few faces, puzzled over a handful more, then waved blindly and quickly when Fran called his name.

Gone again.

Back again.

Gone, and his head began to feel tight from the din, his stomach empty in spite of the ice cream. It was time to go, there was nothing here for him, and once again the urge to weep made him close his eyes as he turned to leave.

"Hey, watch where you're going!"

He stepped back hastily, collided with someone who pushed him away, collided with someone else who wanted to know if he was drunk, and nearly fell over the waist-high iron rail that separated the oval's dirt track from the rides. A hand grabbed his arm and tugged until he followed, through the crowd until he was clear, in front of a stand that sold beer and soda from huge yellow barrels.

"Sorry," he said, taking a handkerchief from his hip pocket and mopping his face.

"It's okay, I just didn't want to get trampled."

He looked, and felt soft heat begin to climb toward his cheeks.

A woman stood next to him, strawberry blonde and nearly as tall as he; her white shirt was open three buttons down, the tails tied over her bare midriff, and her white shorts were high enough to show him muscular tanned legs too smooth to be real. She smiled, hooked one sandaled foot behind the other and folded her arms across her chest.

"You're not drunk, are you?"

He shook his head.

She nodded as the carousel wound down, the music slow-ing, stopping, pausing only a few seconds before starting up again to warn potential riders there wasn't much time.

Casey looked away, afraid she would think he was staring. Which he had been. And cursing himself for not having the glib gift of gab. Standing here like an idiot would chase her away soon enough; the right word, however, just might keep her around a little longer.

The carousel.

Someone screaming delightedly, carried high on a ride.

"Would you like to dance?"

He looked back, but she wasn't laughing. Her right hand pointed at the dance floor.

"Do you speak English?"

"I'm a postman," he answered, and grimaced. "That is, yes. I mean, I speak English, yes."

Her nod forced the blush higher.

"And I guess so," he added. "Dance, I mean. I mean, I'm not very good at it, I haven't danced in years, but—"

"Good enough."

She seized his hand and pulled him, forcing him to follow lest he be yanked off his feet. As it was, he nearly fell twice, tripped over a baby-carriage wheel once, and hopped for a dozen clumsy yards before he regained his balance. By the time they reached the dance floor she was laughing so hard there were tears in the corners of her eyes, and he was ready to be furious, humiliated, and exhilarated.

He had no time to choose.

As soon as their feet touched the wood, she was in his arms and they were dancing. Awkwardly at first, until their bodies adjusted; not perfectly, but smoothly, once they locked on the music's rhythm.

The weight of her left hand on his shoulder was so light he could barely feel it, the warmth of her back through the shirt moved his hand around as if he didn't know how to hold her. He didn't look at her face; he didn't dare, or he'd kick her, or trip her, or step on her toes.

But she did look at him. He could feel it as he watched the others gliding around them, some of them faster, some of them slower, most of them smiling self-consciously or laughing as if it wasn't their idea, to dance in front of their friends, in front of strangers.

Around, like the carousel, until the music stopped.

She curtsied prettily, without mocking.

He bowed as gallantly as he knew how, and asked if she'd like sit down for a while, until he caught his second wind.

"I—"

"There." He pointed at the saddled animals. "At least I won't black-and-blue your poor shins."

She closed one eye in a frozen wink, giggled, and nodded, and they jumped onto the platform just as it began to move. The animals and a few sleighs were three deep, and she hopped onto a stately giraffe, grabbed his shoulder when he tried to climb onto the beast beside her.

"No, the other one," she said, pointing to the inside, a haughty llama with bared teeth.

Puzzled but afraid to argue, he did as he was told, then asked why without speaking.

The carousel began to turn; he grabbed the brass pole as the llama began to rise in a slight forward motion.

"It's a contest," she explained, not quite shouting over the music. "You have to wait for the penny tune."

"Huh?"

Oh, brilliant, Casey, just brilliant, you jackass.

"That's all right." She tilted her head. "See, you can't ride the lion unless you hear the right tune."

"Lion?"

She nodded.

He felt like a jerk for not noticing the creature between them—a male lion. Gold, features suggested rather than carved. It took him so long, he couldn't help thinking of the way he had teased Yard, back at the Brass Ring. But this woman wasn't he; she simply waited until he said, "Oh, I get it. Kind of like musical chairs."

"Right!" She laughed and applauded.

"You hear the tune, you get to the lion first?"

"Right!" she said again, and leaned across the lion's saddle, patted his arm in congratulations. "Ride the lion, win the prize."

"What's the tune? What's the prize?"

A shrug. "It's different every night. Both of them." She pulled away slowly. "So you keep trying, because sometimes it's worth a lot of money."

"Damn, I never heard of it."

She lifted a shoulder. "Who cares, if we win."

Faster, the carnival a blur, the lights a single stream, making him dizzy, and he looked at the mirrors instead, spotting a break in them midway along. An alcove, and in it a quartet of mechanical bears playing drums, horn, chimes, a two-tiered silver xylophone. They wore tuxedos and huge goofy grins; and he soon grinned with them, looked at the woman and wondered when it was he had died and had been carried secretly to heaven, tried to see ahead and behind in hopes that Yard was still around. Yet it didn't matter when he couldn't find his friend because this was somehow something he didn't think he could share.

The carousel slowed, the music slowed with it, and before it was done, she was out of her saddle and off the platform, on the dirt. With a pat to the llama's neck, he climbed down and stood next to her, not sure what to do with his hands, found at least one thing when Fran and her friends raced past him to get back in line, and she waved. He waved back, blew her a kiss.

"Yours?"

"Nope. Just a kid I know." He sniffed, tugged at an earlobe. "Do you work here?"

"Now what makes you think that?"

"I don't recognize you. I mean, it's not that I know everyone in the Station, but—"

She grinned, scowled mockingly, grinned a second time. "Most of the time I substitute at the midway games. You know—a guy needs a break, I step in, stuff like that." A glance and grimace at her watch. "In fact, damnit, I'd better get going or I'm gonna get killed."

"I'll walk with you."

She shook her head, half-turned as if to run. "Too long. Maybe tomorrow, okay?"

He held up a hand. "Hey, wait, what's your name? I can't thank you for the dance and ride if you don't tell me your name."

"Sure you can," she said, and skipped a few steps backward before laughing, spinning, waving with both hands over her head and slipping into the crowd.

He followed rapidly after her for several yards, eventually trying to run and failing, telling himself he was too damn old for this sort of thing, that she had to be at least fifteen years younger than he, with a boyfriend who had muscles growing out of his ears.

Nevertheless he grinned as he slowed, whistled as he left the fair, clapped his hands and punched the air when he heard the fireworks begin. Walking backward along Chancellor Avenue, he watched a rocket explode into a white blossom, a green star, a red shower of sparks. Facing forward was an effort, and he took his time getting home, thinking every so often that she was following him back there, ducking behind trees, crouching behind a hedge, kneeling beside a parked car and stifling her giggles with her hands.

Too old, he told himself, and didn't believe a word.

Swarthy men dressed in black, picking up papers blown by the wind, stuffing them in sacks slung over their shoulders; a second group feeding animals prowling in wheeled cages, the sound of raw meat slapping the bars, hitting the floors; a third group winding through the quiet rides, picking up coins and wallets and pens and combs and stuffing them into sacks slung over their shoulders.

A lone man on the carousel, rag in hand, cleaning the wood, the mirrors, the brass, the iron stirrups; a woman in a windbreaker checking each animal's eyes, legs, necks, hooves, stroking manes and flanks, whispering, moving on; a dark figure on the roof, changing all the lights to blue.

Sunrise; nothing moved.

A horse whickered.

A donkey brayed.

Dust in a brown cloud sifted down the midway.

Casey lay on his bed and connected the cracks in the plaster ceiling into images of planets, galaxies, railroad tracks snaking through mountains, arroyos cutting through a drought-ridden desert. He didn't want to get up. Vacations were for sleeping late, eating poorly, and sooner or later getting down on his knees in the garden. But today, although it was already close to noon and his stomach had begun to growl, he couldn't bring himself to move.

The woman.

He saw her when he closed his eyes, saw her when he rolled over, saw her ghostlike in the corner when he got up in the middle of the night to quench a sudden rasping thirst.

He didn't know her name.

An hour ago the telephone had rung a dozen times before stopping. It hadn't been her. He knew it. She wasn't the type to call. He knew that too. But neither did he believe she was the type who picked strange men out of a crowd and asked them to dance, on a whim. He didn't know why he felt that. She could easily be a Travelers shill, a calculating temptress designed to lure him back to the fair each night, promising without promising while he emptied his pockets and filled his dreams. She could also be a thief setting up a mark. Or nothing more than a tease who fed on the lonely and moved on, not thinking about what moving on left behind.

Funny, he thought, hands rubbing his bare chest; he hadn't really considered himself very lonely until last night. First Tina and her bitchy friend, then all the music and lights and Fran and the rest . . . It wasn't that he felt sorry for himself, though god knows he went through that particular nonsense from time to time. It was just that he hadn't quite counted, in his youth, on spending his thirties marking time alone.

Molly said midlife crisis.

Hell, maybe she was right.

Hell, maybe he was going through some kind of change, something biological maybe, or something cooking along unknown up in his brain.

Hell, maybe so.

And if that was true, so what if he wasn't a millionaire by now, surrounded by family and family retainers; so what if he wasn't ensconced in a home with traditional ivy and roses, bouncing babies on his knees; so what?

Did that mean he was a failure?

His pillow was punched twice and finally tossed aside.

He didn't know.

The hell of it was, he just didn't know.

The telephone again; he sighed and sat up, scratched chest and belly and took his time getting into the living room, dropping onto the couch, picking up the receiver.

It was Tina, barely giving him a hello before launching into an effusive apology for the way her friend had acted in the bar. Still not fully awake, and slightly embarrassed that he was practically naked, he allowed her to continue while he wondered why she cared. He certainly didn't give a damn. It was a truly sad thing about Norma's husband dying the way he had, but he hadn't liked her when the poor guy was alive, why should that change now?

"So," Tina said breathlessly, "I hope you're not mad."

"Not me." He picked at something on his knee.

"Good." She actually sounded relieved.

"Yeah." He looked at his feet, wriggled his toes. "You at school?"

"On break. You get them a lot in summer school. We can only stand so much, if you know what I mean."

"Oh. Yeah."

Voices in the background; the muffled clang of a bell.

"Oh hell," she said. "Fire drill. I hate these damn things. Hey, maybe I'll see you tonight, huh? You going to the fair?"

"Yes," he answered before he could stop himself.

"Great," she said. "Maybe I'll see you."

"Sure," he said, but she'd already gone, and he sat for a while, listening to the house, before deciding it was time to take a shower and join the living. Then lunch while he was still wrapped in his towel, rinsed the dishes and dressed in shorts cut from an old pair of chinos. A baseball cap for the sun. Gloves caked with old dirt. A metal pail on the back stoop that held his hand tools.

His home was small, a single-story clapboard cottage blocked against his neighbors by a screen of closely spaced poplars. A private world to protect his ladies, his flowers. He didn't name them, but he talked to them, and by killing them and crippling them and nursing them and feeding them, he learned that time would pass, and he could mark it by their blossoms.

He decided to work in the garden first, a large rectangle he had cleared in the center of the yard. A bitch of a job because there had been more stones under the surface than in any quarry he had seen. It had taken him one entire summer, but by god it had been worth it.

The procedure was all automatic: Plop the pail down, turn on the hose and drag it out with the nozzle shut to a dripping, smooth the grass and kneel, check the sky, crack his knuckles, then examine the flower bed to give him his first chore.

"Son of a bitch," he said. "God damn son of a bitch."

The flowers—marigolds and snapdragons, peonies and pansies, irises in the center—were all dead.

"No," he whispered, looked away and looked back, but nothing had changed. The blossoms had wilted, the stems drying to brown stalks, and the rich black earth so carefully mixed and loosened was dry and cracked.

"I . . . what . . ."

On hands and knees he circled the bed, testing the ground outside the rim, rapping the ground inside, finally rocking back on his heels and covering his mouth with one hand.

There was nothing wrong with the lawn; only the garden had died.

"How?"

He stood, dropped the gloves, checked all the shrubs planted near the trees and along the back; checked the foundation rose garden on the left side of the house, checked the garden in front, the one that framed the narrow porch, and saw nothing wrong, nothing to alarm him.

"How?"

He knew he hadn't neglected anything, especially not the watering, and though he might miss a day or two weeding and put off a transplanting here and there, it had never been long enough to create such a disaster. He would have had to have left it alone all season, even covering it from the rain.

"How? God damn, how?"

In a near panic then, he set up all his sprinklers and let them spin, checking to make sure every corner, every inch, every blade and leaf was touched by the mist. Then he took a trowel to the back garden, turned the earth over, holding it close to his eyes, sifting it between his fingers, once even going so far as to bring some to his tongue. The roots were brittle, there were no signs of grubs or worms, beetles or ants.

The ground was dead.

He called a nursery out on Mainland Road, down the hill near Harley, but they couldn't tell him a thing from just his descriptions; he called Yard at the hardware store, but Chase wasn't much of a gardener—his sympathies were genuine, but his mind was on business; and with no one else to talk to, he dumped a handful of the dirt into a paper bag and brought it to Adelle Vanders at The Florist, on Centre Street.

"Amazing," she said, emptying the bag onto a worktable in her back room. "Casey, how the hell did you manage this?"

"I didn't," he answered sharply. "Damnit, you know me better than that."

The portly white-haired woman slipped on a pair of half glasses and leaned over the table as far as her smock-dressed bulk would allow. Poked thoughtfully at the dirt, dribbled some water on it from a small can, and finally shook her head in defeat. "This is the deadest stuff I've ever seen outside a desert, and even that has some life. Case, you must have done something. A pesticide, maybe?"

His hands clenched at his sides. "Adelle, that dirt there, it was fine only two days ago. Mulch, loam, everything, and—"

"Impossible." She straightened and took off her glasses. "Casey, you know as well as I do that nothing like this could happen in that short a time."

He opened his mouth to brand her a liar, saw the hurt in her expression, and practically ran out of the shop. She didn't call him back; he didn't have the nerve to return. Instead he walked, nearly ran, back to the house and turned off the sprinklers. Went in through the front door and stood in the kitchen, stared out the window.

The grass glinted, droplets clung to some of the trees' lower branches, a robin hopped from shade to shade, cocking its head as if it were listening for its prey.

The garden was barren, a scorch mark on the lawn.

All right, he thought; all right, so Adelle doesn't know, that doesn't mean she knows everything. You put some more in a bag and you take it to the college. One of the professors there will tell you, they can check it in their lab.

He nodded.

He didn't move.

He watched the robin fly away without going near the bare earth, watched shade become shadow, remembered all the work he had done to give the yard color.

Casey, oh Casey, how does your garden grow?

He looked at his hands, at the dirt beneath the nails and in the cracks of his knuckles. Poisoned, he thought suddenly; dear god, it had been poisoned. He ran for the bathroom, stripped and threw his clothes into the wastebasket under the sink, stood under the hot water and scrubbed his flesh scarlet. Then he shoved the shower curtain aside and sat on the edge of the tub, taking deep breaths until he knew he wouldn't die.

Clean clothes made him feel better. A can of soup stopped his stomach from complaining before it started. And as he stacked the dishes in the sink, he heard himself whistling the song he'd heard the night before.

"Casey would waltz," he sang, "with the strawberry blonde . . ."

God, he was terrible.

". . . and the band played on."

He was truly horrible.

"He waltzed 'cross the floor with the girl he adored . . ."

Jesus.

He couldn't hold a tune in an iron bucket, but he laughed as he left the kitchen, sobered for an instant when he thought of the dead flowers, then laughed again and decided that another night at the fair would clear his head, help him think, and first thing in the morning he'd go out to the college.

He laughed again as he locked the front door.

"Clear your head?" he said to the twilight. "Christ, Bethune, who the hell do you think you're kidding?"

She wasn't there.

He walked the length of the crowded midway and its side streets several times, ate more than he should have to give his hands something to do, ended up at the carousel and called himself ten kinds of a fool and a hundred kinds of an idiot who ought to be old enough to know better.

She wasn't there.

He rode on a dolphin and a ram, watched the bears play their tunes, tried to catch himself in the mirrors; he stood by the dance floor and tapped his foot, nodded his head, snapped his fingers, turned and watched the thrill-rides until a threatened headache closed his eyes.

She wasn't there.

He drifted past a Ferris wheel that seemed to wobble on its

braces; he listened to a jovial barker try to convince passersby that inside his tent, and nowhere else in the world, was the only living survivor of a mysterious tribe of African pygmies, who ate only roots and berries and a pound of human flesh a day; on the midway he tried to knock down a three-level pyramid of milk bottles until he gave up in disgust; he spotted Tina Elby with some friends at a hamburger stand and made an abrupt about-face into a wide lane that boasted farm and jungle animal exhibits, with a small arena at the far end where the acts for an hourly show were posted.

Twice, he started to leave, disgusted with himself for acting like an adolescent, and twice changed his mind. Just in case.

He returned to the carousel and rode the llama four times.

No one rode the gold lion.

He headed for the exit, ignoring the crowds, ignoring the music, ripping the ticket from his shirt and tearing it in half, tossing it over his shoulder and not caring when someone behind him complained about the slob.

She didn't promise, you know, he said to the toes of his dust-covered shoes; she only said maybe.

Shit.

Damn.

He stood under the arch and glared across the Road at the Station, daring someone, anyone, to say the wrong thing so he could smash in a face, kick in a few ribs, spend the night in jail and it would serve them all right.

She called his name.

He turned abruptly and tripped over his own feet, stumbled backward and tried to wave as she rode by on a palomino pony, a gang of kids in cowboy suits running behind and cheering.

"Tomorrow!" she called as she veered into the midway. "After sunset!"

He grinned; he waved.

He nodded; he grinned.

He hummed all the way home and fell asleep on the couch, woke up with a stiff neck and hummed in the shower, got into fresh working clothes and slapped his thighs as if he were slapping leather.

"All right, boys," he said to his tools in a cowboy drawl, "there's some heavy work on the south forty gotta be done before sunset." He stepped out onto the front porch. "Head 'em up, move 'em out."

All the shrubbery was brown, all the flowers shriveled.

A stout bar across the entrance, a quintet of crows perched on the weathered black wood, facing the road, every few minutes fluffing feathers, stretching wings, pecking at drying strings of red meat draped over the barrier.

Hammering inside, the whine of a saw.

Sun bright, heat strong, no one to take tickets because no one had come and no one would come, though there was no sign on the arch that declared the fair closed; later, much later, but for now just the crows.

And from somewhere inside, the soft quiet sound of a young woman laughing.

He stood on the front walk, hands first in his hip pockets, then on his hips, then clasped, clenched, back in his pockets, tangled behind his back, shredding blades of grass, adjusting his belt. He didn't know what to do and so did and said nothing as a uniformed woman knelt beside the porch steps and scraped something into a clear plastic bag. It was the fifth time she'd done it. Maybe the sixth. He'd lost count. And he had stopped trying to talk to her because all he had received thus far for his efforts had been grunts and a maddeningly professional, don't-worry-about-it smile.

She said her name was Trudy. Officer Iverson. Fair hair in a thick braid at the back of her head, a minimum of makeup, not much of a figure though he'd fought not to wince when she'd shaken his hand.

A footstep behind him, but he didn't turn. If it was one more goddamn neighbor asking one more damnfool question, he would scream; he would tear off someone's head; he would print up flyers and pass them around so they'd leave him the hell alone while his land died around him.

The footstep passed on.

Iverson rose, dusted her knees, tucked the bag into a pocket of her tunic. "That should do it."

He waited.

She glanced around, shaking her head helplessly. "Tell you the truth, Mr. Bethune, I haven't the slightest idea what this is all about."

"Well, it has to be some kind of poison," he insisted, as he had when she'd first arrived, not ten minutes after he'd called the station. "Things—plants, I mean—just don't die like that, not that fast, not practically overnight, for god's sake." He looked for sympathy; she gave him a shrug. "Somebody did it. It didn't happen by itself."

Lips pulled, almost a smile. "We'll let you know as soon as we can."

"When?"

"I don't know. We'll call."

Hands waved impotently. "And what am I supposed to do now?"

She passed him, paused, bowed her head for a moment before patting the place where the bag had disappeared. "Mr. Bethune, all I can say is, don't try to plant anything new in any of those places until we can find out what was used to destroy your flowers." Her tone told him she didn't think this was a police matter at all; his expression told her that this many plants cost one hell of a lot of money, which postmen don't have to throw around, in case she hadn't noticed. "Give us a call on Monday—"

"Monday!"

"—and maybe we'll have your answer. Take it easy." A last look. "Good thing nobody's pet was around."

Right, he thought; it's only a damn flower, hell, at least it's not a dog, god forbid.

After she disappeared around the corner, he went inside and sat in the kitchen until he couldn't stand it anymore, walked through every room until he wanted to scream, grabbed his wallet from the dresser and walked to the Brass Ring just after it opened. Molly wasn't on duty yet, and for that he was grateful. He didn't think he could stand her commiseration, her sad smiles, or her off-the-cuff psychology lectures.

He drank slowly until supper, walked extra carefully across the street to the Luncheonette, had a sandwich and strong coffee, waited until he was sure he wouldn't fall, then returned to the bar.

Drank while he listened to Oxley explain to a newcomer the finer points of playing darts without putting a hole or two in one's foot.

Stared at the walls, the ceiling, swiveled around and looked out at the street. But the faces passing by were indistinct, grey, and he turned away to watch the bartender wipe off the tables.

He blinked several times, quite slowly, and tried to release his breath, suddenly caught in his lungs.

"Hey," he said quietly to the glass in his hand.

and he's a creep, a so-called man who talks to stupid goddamn flowers

"Hey."

nothing but goddamn weeds

In order to keep from bolting, and screaming, he placed money and glass on the bar with exaggerated deliberation, waved his usual farewell and strolled outside, where he leaned immediately and heavily against the wall when the sun blared in his eyes and set a painfully slow dervish working in his head. Not good. This wouldn't do. Wouldn't do at all. He had to be sober when he . . . no, maybe he wouldn't go to the police. To Iverson the Iron Bitch, who would most likely tell him that words don't mean much when they're grumbled in a bar, and they certainly weren't a threat.

How the hell, Mr. Bethune, do you threaten a rose?

He swallowed, rubbed his mouth, and coughed into a fist.

People on the sidewalk glanced at him, or ignored him, but none of them stopped to ask what was wrong.

He chuckled to himself—he was practically invisible. The postman is drunk, folks, so pretend he's not there. What the hell, that should be easy, they do it when he's sober.

He swallowed again and held his breath, released it in spurts, and pushed away from the building, heading south, heading home where he could dig out the telephone book and see where Hobbs lived. He doubted she had flowers. He doubted she even had a yard. She probably stayed in a boardinghouse and bossed the landlady around.

He made it as far as the corner of his block before he had to stop and prop a shoulder against a lamppost. Deep breaths.

Swallowing. Walking once more, not quite straight, not quite staggering, glancing at the houses he passed, knowing that the woman in there has trouble with her medical bills, the family over there subscribes to nine magazines and two out-of-state newspapers, the unmarried couple in the place across from his receives letters from France at least twice a month. He knew them, he thought as he turned to look back the way he had come; he knew them all and knew them well and didn't know them at all unless he had an envelope in his hand.

"Oh god," he said. "Oh god."

He bypassed his front door, went around the side into the shade.

The roses were dead, petals strewn on the ground, fluttering in a breeze as if trying to crawl to the grass.

He dropped to his knees, hands weak on his thighs, counting the bushes, reaching out and grabbing a stem, snatching his hand back and staring dumbly at the blood bubbles welling in his palm. There was no pain. Just the blood. He sucked at the punctures while he looked up at the house and saw, below one window beneath the eaves, a long blister of white paint pulling away from the wood. Higher, and there was another, just under the gutter, a section of which had somehow worked loose from its bracket.

This wasn't right.

This couldn't be happening.

But he was too befuddled to think straight and so didn't try. He crawled instead on all fours into the backyard, shook his head once at the spectacle he was and shoved himself grunting to his feet, climbed the stoop, banged open the kitchen door and tripped over the threshold as he went in.

He hung on to the nearest counter and lowered his head until it cleared. Cold shower. What he needed a long, cold, stinging shower, a gallon or two of hot coffee, clean clothes and some food—in that order. After that, he'd hunt down Norma and . . . he rubbed his eyes, his temples, decided he would cross that bridge when he came to it. As it was, unless he sobered up, he'd probably kill himself first.

A laugh.

He began to strip as he headed for the bathroom.

". . . waltz 'cross the floor," he sang, badly and loudly and not giving a damn, "with the girl he adored . . ."

Right, he thought; right!

She wanted to see him tonight.

How the hell could he have forgotten? A beautiful young woman had made a date with him, and it had completely slipped his mind. And there, he scolded himself, is the reason, you jackass, why you're not rich, why you don't have a love life, why you ain't never going to be more than a carrier all your life—you don't believe the good things even when they drop on your thick, fat skull. Jackass is right. You got to be clobbered with a two-by-four before anyone can get your attention.

All right. Well, she had his attention now.

Yard called while he was eating: "Heard you tied one on this afternoon, m'friend."

"Nigel has a big mouth."

A television shouted the evening news in the background, until someone else shouted to turn the damn thing down.

Casey grinned, took another bite of his steak.

"So, hey," Yard said, "you okay?"

"Yeah. Sort of."

"Sort of." An intentionally loud sigh. "So look, the family's going to the Travelers tonight, rumor saying it being the last and all. You want to come along? Be glad to have you. I need someone to tell me what the tricks are."

"Very funny."

"Maybe we'll bump into the teacher."

Casey looked at the back door and saw a rose petal on the floor, curled, a baby's fist. "Dead," he said quietly.

"What? She is?"

"My garden, Yard. The last one."

"Oh Jesus."

"I got home and all the roses were dead. And are you ready for this? Even the paint's starting to come off the walls outside."

"Can't be. We worked for three days, that paint's on there for life."

"It's coming off, Yard. I swear it, it's coming off."

"We'll check it tomorrow. First thing. Some damp might have gotten underneath it."

"Sure. Okay."

"So look, Case, are you coming—"

"Hey, Yard?"

"What?"

"Do you know what a penny tune is?"

"Never heard of it. You sure you're still not a little in a bag there?"

Casey hung up, gathered his plates and dropped them in the sink. Then he picked up the petal and dropped it into the trash can. The wall clock—hands and numerals in the belly of a crowing rooster—told him it was already past seven. An hour to kill before the sun went down, then a check in the mirror to be sure he was still human, and off to the fair.

The telephone rang.

Christ, he thought as he slapped up the receiver; nobody calls for two weeks, then everybody calls.

It was Tina.

"Listen," she said, speaking rapidly, her voice nervous, "Norma and I are going to the carnival tonight and we thought maybe you'd like to come with us? I mean, she's feeling pretty bad about what she said the other day, she wants to make it up to you, buy you a hot dog or something? I thought maybe if you were going..."

Waltz 'cross the floor.

"Damn, Tina," he said, "I'm really sorry but I already have ... that is, I'm already meeting someone."

"Oh." Silence, but not long. "Well, hey, that's fine, that's great. Anybody we know?"

He felt suddenly awkward, almost defensive. "No, I don't think so."

"Oh. Okay. Well, maybe we'll see you there, okay?"

"Sure. Probably."

"And Casey," she said, "Norma really is sorry."

Waltz 'cross the floor, all the roses are dead.

"I doubt it, Tina," he said flatly, and hung up.

She was there.

The midway was crowded, all the concessions busy, but he saw her the moment he stepped into the oval. She was on the Octopus, alone, hair yanked and tossed by the ride's private wind. He stood back and watched her, grinning, waving once when she spotted him and raised her hands in a boxer's victory salute. For a moment he didn't want her to come down, and didn't watch her until she'd reached the top of each arc. She was among the stars; she was a star; she was, he thought with an abrupt tightening across his chest, his own star, nameless and distant no matter how close she came to touching the ground.

A woman walked by, a rose in her hair.

The roses are dead.

His brow broke sweat in warm running beads, and when the strawberry blonde was momentarily lost to view, he tried to spot Tina and the poisoning bitch in the crowd, whose faces were frozen in manic grins and widened eyes. And in failing, failed to notice that the Octopus had lowered its arms until he looked back and couldn't find her.

Damn, he thought in near panic, and raised himself on his toes. But he was too short to look over heads and so forced himself to wait, half praying, half fearful, sagging at last when she broke around a man following his paunch around the track.

He grinned.

She smiled, leaned over and kissed his cheek.

"Corri," she whispered, hands holding his shoulders, his own hands fluttering, not knowing where to go. "Corri Pilgrim."

His mouth opened; she closed it with a finger.

"You wanted to know my name," she reminded him, slipped an arm around his waist and nudged him into moving.

"Oh." His own arm and her waist; she didn't pull away. "You the boss's daughter or something?"

"We're all Pilgrims here."

He stared.

She winked. "That's supposed to be a joke."

"Oh." She felt soft, hot without discomfort, hip against hip. "Oh."

Clockwise around the oval.

"You don't feel right, Casey," she said, head tilting and quickly touching his cheek. "Are you sad?"

"Not anymore."

A shy glance at the ground. "But you were?"

"I guess. Yes."

He told her about the past two days, about the destruction of his gardens and all the unsuccessful attempts to discover the reasons; he tried to make light of his suspicions of Norma Hobbs, but he could hear the hate prowling around the edge of his voice and it startled him, quieted him for a moment, until she hugged him as they walked and said that what he needed, tonight, wasn't a solution but an evasion.

"A what?"

They paused at a stand to buy cans of soda, stood to one side to drink and watched a hard-tested mother coax a young boy from the cab of a tiny train engine, but he was having none of it. He wanted to ride. He didn't want to give up pulling the cord that rang the bell or pushing the green button that tooted the steam whistle.

"Sometimes," Corri said, "it doesn't pay to fight."

He thought she was talking about the woman and the child until he felt her looking at him. A brief scowl as they walked away, hand in hand this time.

"You're not suggesting I forget about my flowers?"

No answer.

"I can't do that. Really. I mean, if the lack of rain had killed them, my neglect, something like that, I'd feel like hell, but I wouldn't give up gardening. Hell, you can always plant more, in a case like that. But this . . . this wasn't my fault. Somebody . . ." A shuddering deep breath. Her hand tightened around his. "Somebody deliberately . . . it's like they came into my house and stole everything I owned that meant something whether it was valuable or not." He rubbed his brow. "I'm sorry, I'm not making much sense."

"You are," she said, twirled around in front of him, stopping him while she kissed him again. On the lips. Sweet candy and warm breezes, a hint of strawberry when his amazement finally allowed him to kiss her back.

"Well," he said when they were done.

Nobody looked.

A train whistle sounded.

"Sometimes," she whispered, lips close to his ear, "it's all right to run away, even for just a while."

He didn't know, didn't understand.

"It clears your head." Lips at the other ear. "Lets you think. Like counting to ten, Casey. It's like counting to ten."

"Ah. Okay. So when I see that bitch I won't tear off her head before I say hello."

"Something like that."

Still close, not moving, nobody looking.

"So." He gestured to gather the fair in. "This is my evasion?"

She shook her head, winked, led him around the track until he saw the carousel. "Maybe we'll get lucky tonight."

A quick look this time, but there was nothing in her expression to tell him what she meant. If, he thought with a flush of guilt, she meant anything at all.

They stood in line. Held hands. Didn't speak as the carousel turned and the line moved and the cacophony of the fair settled into a buzzing that was soon no sound at all.

Evasion.

He supposed that was a natural response for someone who lived with a carnival that seldom stayed in one place for more than a week or two at a time. Don't worry about problems; next Monday they'll still be here but we won't. Our lights will blind you, and while you're rubbing your eyes we slip out of town.

The carousel turned, animals and riders sweeping forward, up and down.

Dead roses, dead paint.

It was as if, he thought with a start, the Station was rejecting him. Slice by slice, carving him away from whatever he knew, whatever he had.

The idea terrified him, and he gripped Corri's hand more tightly.

But what if it were true? What if his presence here was no longer required, what if he had fulfilled his function and was now being eased out? Dead roses. Dead paint. He and Yard had worked for days scraping and patching and replacing and painting and trimming and wiping up. Last fall. Last September. The paint couldn't be dead. But neither could the roses.

The carousel stopped.

The riders scrambled off, waving, pretending to be dizzy, some racing back along the track to get on the end of the line.

Casey felt a tug and stumbled forward.

"Come on," Corri urged. "Our lucky night, remember?"

He climbed onto the platform, into the pale-green light, and followed her, weaving through the frozen bestiary until they found the llama and the giraffe. His foot fumbled with the stirrup, his palms were unaccountably slick, and, shamefaced, he was about to give up and ask for a boost. Then it worked, and he was on, grinning at the grinning bears on their bandstand to his left. They shuddered, a bell rang, and the carousel began to move as the bears began to play.

Up, and he saw straight ahead a huge billy goat, head tilted to the right, roses carved into its beard.

Down, and he saw his smeared reflection in the pole, covered it with his hand, looked quickly right and saw his face in the lion's saddle.

Corri waved at him.

He blew her a kiss.

Abruptly the music stopped, nothing now but the creak of gears and the hiss of the wind.

He held his breath for a second, fearing the ride had broken down, that the rest of his turns would be spent listening to nothing but the machine below the magic. A quizzical look to Corri, but he couldn't see her face because beyond her, in the fair, nothing moved, nothing stirred. He was going up, going down, had to squint in the wind his passing created, but outside, on the oval, everything had frozen.

A single note from a xylophone.

Corri pursed her lips and kissed the air. "I knew it!" she cried, and gestured frantically at the lion.

He couldn't move.

A single beat of a drum.

"Hurry!" she called. "Casey, hurry!"

A horn played two notes; chimes played two more.

Up and down.

Awkwardly, keeping a one-handed grip on her pole, she leaned over and snatched at his sleeve, tried to pull him out of his seat. "Damnit, Casey, come on, move!"

But nothing moved.

Three notes, four beats.

He wiped his hands on his shirt, felt a twinge and examined his palms. Red dots where the thorns had pricked him; on the other side, lines of garden earth in the lines of his knuckles. For what? he wondered.

A firm grip on his arm pulled until he had to slap a hand on the lion's back to keep from falling. Corri glared at him, urged him, while the lion flew up and down between them.

"I can't do it, I work here," she said, desperation around her eyes. "Please, Casey, before the band plays."

He was afraid.

It was stupid, he knew it, but he couldn't help feeling a touch of ice in the air that made him blink rapidly, as if casting snow from his lashes.

"Let go of the damn pole, swing your leg over."

So what would he win if he did?

Would it bring back the roses and make the paint fresh again? Would it somehow, magically, give him a larger paycheck, put him first in line for the postmaster job? Would it prevent the Station from tossing him aside?

It might, something answered; what the hell, it just might.

He nodded.

She laughed.

With much twisting and near slipping, in a move he was sure was laughable to those who watched, he transferred to the back of the sinking gold lion, grabbed on, held on, as the beast rose and the lights flared and the band played its song as if it had never been interrupted.

Corri cheered.

Casey laughed.

He raised his arms in triumph and looked around to see how many others knew what he'd done. Yard would have a fit; it would be great to see the look on his face.

The carousel was empty.

"Hey, Corri—"

She was gone.

Behind him, the animals rose and fell, rose and fell, forever charging and never closing mouths frozen open, eyes wide and blind, rising, and falling, leaning close, and away; before him, they fled, hooves and paws and tails and manes, rising, and falling, never quite reaching the turn in the bend.

The band played a little faster.

The carousel turned a little faster.

"Corri!"

God damn, he'd been tricked. She was a shill after all, some kind of gag played on the local yokel and everyone out there having a good laugh at his expense. He glared out toward the oval, ready to tell them he didn't think it was funny, but the glare disappeared when he saw nothing but the night beyond the fall of green light.

No lights, no rides, no people—only what looked like a vast field, and a vast field of stars out there on the horizon.

The band played.

The carousel turned.

Off, he ordered then; get the hell off, find out who's in charge and get the bitch fired.

He couldn't.

As much as he tried, his feet wouldn't leave the stirrups, and as much as he lunged side to side, back and forth, he couldn't lift off the saddle. Frantically, then, he shoved and pushed and kicked and punched, until something stabbed a muscle at the base of his spine, until his arms wilted at his sides and his legs wouldn't obey.

Ride it out, then; wait for the joke to end.

Rising.

Falling.

Wait. All you have to do is wait. They won't leave you here to starve or die of thirst. Sooner or later they'll shut down, have their laugh, and you can go home. Tend the gardens. Repaint the house. Fix the gutter. Give Tina a call and take her to dinner. Maybe—he smiled weakly—you could apologize to Norma for wanting to kill her.

Rising.

It won't be long.

Falling.

It can't be long.

Close your eyes, he suggested, and pretend it's all a dream, just like in the movies.

The carousel turned.

His eyes wouldn't close. He had to look—ahead and behind, in case they were hiding someplace; out in the field, in case someone turned on the lights. He had to listen—to the music, to know when it began to slow down, when the bears stopped playing that same goddamn tune.

Oh god, Casey thought; dear God, he prayed.

"Oh god!" Casey screamed as the animals charged and fled, as the mirrors winked and darkened, as the stars never changed, as the night didn't lighten, as he heard above the thunder of the carousel as it turned the soft quiet sound of a young woman, laughing.

He rode through the night without the strawberry blonde.

And the band played on.

II

Will You Be Mine?

THE WORLD CHANGED WHEN THE CARTONS WERE ALL emptied, crushed, dragged out to the curb for the garbage truck to take away. Before, when dishes were still being unwrapped, when the toys were still jumbled in their boxes, when all the good clothes were still crammed into their hanging bags with the stuck zippers and probably forever wrinkled, there had still been a chance her parents would change their minds. They would see that this house wasn't as nice as their real home, that the town was too small for anything to happen worth getting up for, that the people just weren't the same as the ones she had left behind. They would see that, they would understand, they would say *oops, sorry, fran, we blew it,* get into the car and drive away without looking back.

Still a chance.

Even when the moving van had backed out of the driveway and pulled away, coughing smoke and grinding gears, swaying as it rounded the corner and disappeared.

Even when Daddy had carried Mom kicking and giggling over the threshold.

Still a chance.

Until the cartons were empty.

The worst day of her life.

A warm day, with flowers and bees and bluejays and cars with their windows rolled down, trailing music behind them; a T-shirt and jeans and sneakers and dark hair like her father's, just long enough to poke at her eyes when the breeze snuck up on her from around the side of the house.

She sat on the front porch on an upturned orange crate and propped her elbows on the railing that needed a coat of paint, her cheeks in her palms, glaring at the street half in sunlight, half in shade. All those trees. All those houses. All those hedges taller than she was. Old. Everything was old and big and she supposed it was nice enough for the people who had to live here, but it wasn't home. And it wasn't ever going to be.

She sighed. Loudly. Mournfully. With just a hint of a false sob.

No one heard her; they were too busy unpacking.

She sighed again, this time to herself.

When the breeze blew and things shifted just beyond the range of clear vision, she felt like she was trapped in one of those crazy dreams she got whenever she had a fever. A dream where things had sharp edges, even the pillows, yet nothing ever cut her and she never quite bled and nothing was ever quite in focus. A dream like looking through glitter-laced gauze, where every footstep was a gunshot and every whisper a shout and every color hurt her eyes but didn't make her turn away. Nothing ever made sense in a fever dream—she could fly, she could die, she could carry a tune—and nothing made sense now.

She scratched her cheeks without moving her hands.

Nothing made sense, but this wasn't a dream.

Behind her, she could hear her mother singing something that had no words as she sorted out the stuff that had to hang in the living room, the dining room, the foyer, the hall to the kitchen, while her father carted armfuls of junk upstairs where, in a little while, more sorting would take place. He wasn't singing. He made fun of her mother instead, laughing fun that had them both giggling.

Fran rolled her eyes.

This was nuts.

They were actually *glad* to be here. They actually thought *she* was glad to be here. They actually really and truly believed that this was going to be the greatest thing that ever happened to them in the whole world. She had no idea grown-ups could be so amazingly stupid.

No chance at all.

She didn't bother to sigh; it wouldn't do any good, even when her father joined her, lighting a cigarette, flicking the match to the yard, blowing smoke rings that didn't, this time, make her smile.

"Well!" He leaned against the post, looking down at her. His sleeves were rolled up, pale hairy arms; his shirt was unbuttoned, a pale hairy chest made worse by an uneven V of brown at the hollow of his throat. His hair, black without a shine, clung to the sweat on his forehead. His face, round save for a hooknose Fran prayed she wouldn't get when she got that old, was slightly red. A good red. A working red. "Man, this sure beats that cramped old apartment, doesn't it? Like moving to a palace."

Not quite, she thought sourly, grunted, and squeezed her

cheeks more tightly, the tips of her fingers pressing the flesh against her teeth.

He waved an arm toward the lawn. "Look, Fran—real grass, real bushes, real trees that aren't choked by fumes. Y'know, I could hang a swing from that one by the driveway if you want. You know, a tire on a rope." He blew smoke, smiled. "When I was kid—no wisecracks, please—I used to have a tire swing my dad rigged up, even though my mother thought I'd get killed or hanged or something on it. It was a huge tire, from a truck. It was great. Damn, it was great. Your hands got all black, your bottom got creases—" He laughed. "Great stuff, kiddo, great stuff."

"Sure, Daddy," she muttered.

So what was so great about getting dirty? Every time she did back home, her mother always scolded her. A tire swing would put her into orbit.

The air was still. Warmer. Insects whispered in the shrubs and trees. The smoke from his cigarette hung too long before drifting away.

She didn't make room when he straddled the railing; his right knee touched her left elbow, and felt hot. She didn't look at him, but she could smell him. The Daddy smell—cigarette smoke and hot jeans and sweat and something else that made him only him, no one else. In the dark she knew it was him; from a zillion miles away in a strong wind she knew. Most of the time it was a comforting thing; today it was annoying.

"You don't like it here, huh," he said softly.

She shook her head.

"Scary, right?"

A slight tilt of her head so she could look sideways at his face, show him her scorn. "C'mon, Daddy, it's not scary here."

"I didn't mean that."

They had been through this before, more times than she could count:

i know how it is, fran, honest to god, i do—a new house, new school, meeting new friends, it isn't easy, it's really kind of scary.

i don't want to go.

wish i could help you.

i could stay by myself.

you're only twelve.

that's big enough.

not quite, honey, not quite.

"Well," she insisted quietly, "I'm not scared."

"Okay." He swung his leg back over and stood, puffed on the cigarette and crushed it out against the railing. "You want to give your mother a hand? I'd like to get this over with before you graduate from college."

"Do I have to?"

"Yes, you have to. The sooner we get this done, the sooner you'll be able to settle in."

"I'll be grumpy," she warned.

He laughed, and suddenly grabbed her under the arms and swung her off the crate. High, to the porch roof; low, between his legs; high again and spinning slowly, and despite the scowl she made sure he saw so he'd know he wasn't getting away with it, she couldn't hold it—it slipped into a reluctant smile she shook away as soon as he put her down and planted a loud wet kiss on her brow.

"Go," he said, swatted her bottom, and she went.

Turning off her brain for the rest of the morning, not thinking about how ugly and permanent everything looked already, just putting stuff where it was supposed to belong, even though it didn't belong here at all but back in Cambridge. Then Daddy called for lunch, crawling on hands and knees into the kitchen and begging for food, so they had cheese sandwiches on the back porch, sitting on folding chairs around a rickety card table with paint splatters on it watching some birds fighting, or playing, in the overgrown yard. A large yard. A huge yard.

"That," her father declared, "is going to take a year to clean out. Even if I hired a gardener."

"You'll love it, Neal. It'll give you something to do in your spare time."

"Oh, right," he grumbled.

Her mother winked at Fran and pointed with half a pickle. "It really won't be all that bad, will it? It'll just take a little planning. We can put the new roses over there, see? and transplant some of that lilac to the side of the house, maybe—"

"What did I tell you," he said to Fran. "A year, at least."

She didn't care and wished he'd stop acting as if she did. Roses and lilacs didn't mean a thing. All she saw was a jungle that would probably eat her alive before the summer was over. Prickly old bushes crawling all over a wood fence that looked like a sneeze would bring it down, a couple of big old trees with hardly any leaves, and grass that even from here she could tell would reach up to her knees. With bugs in it. Tons of them. She could see them flying around—gnats and bees and probably monster spiders hiding down by the ground that would gobble her up without bothering to spin a web.

"Lanette, I think our child is plotting an escape."

Fran gaped at him.

Her mother laughed quietly, touched her bare arm. "You've done enough for one day, I think. You want to go exploring?"

She didn't. But she nodded anyway because she didn't

want to work either, and stood patiently by her chair while her mother gently wiped her mouth with a napkin.

"Not far, honey. You don't know all the streets yet."

"I know," she said, and ran through the house, down the front steps, and stopped at the foot of the walk, whose concrete had been shoved up and cracked and split by last winter; something else, her father had said, he'd have to take care of pretty soon, before somebody tripped and broke a leg and sued him to death. Like the bushes along the front, nearly as high as she was and tangled together almost like a hedge. Large leaves and bright berries mixed with tiny leaves on long branches with tiny yellow flowers. It was ugly; it was all ugly and horrible, and before her parents changed their minds, she raced up the street, not looking at the other houses, not looking at the other yards, not looking at anything until she reached the corner.

When she looked back, the new house was gone.

The block twice as long as any she'd ever known had swallowed it in every shade of green she had ever seen in her life.

She grinned, snapped her fingers and whispered, "Yeah!"

She crossed the street and walked this time, picked up a long whip of a branch and lashed viciously at her shadow, at bugs that flew too near, at every bole she passed. She paid no attention to the numbers on the doors or the street signs; she wasn't curious about the voices she heard, either way off in the distance where Daddy said there was a park, or behind some house that looked like the one where the witch caught Hansel and Gretel, only bigger. She turned. She walked. She turned again. Patiently, not bothering to worry about the time. Because sooner or later a policeman would stop her, ask her her name, and when she had to give her address she would give him the one in Cambridge and get all weepy and tell him she was lost and missed her mommy. The policeman would take her home. Not here. There. She would drive all the way across Connecticut in a police car and pull up in front of her apartment building to the cheers of her friends. Her parents would worry for a while, but it wouldn't be long before they'd figure it out. They would follow, they would find her sitting on the steps, waiting, and they would know that they had made the worst mistake in their lives.

She whipped her shadow again, caught herself on the shin, and yelped.

It would never happen.

There wasn't a policeman that dumb in the whole world.

Maybe there was a bus she could take. God, this place had to have a bus, didn't it? She searched her pockets and found nothing but lint.

She was stuck.

No chance at all.

At last the first tear—the one she had beaten back a dozen times since getting out of the motel bed that morning—made its way to her cheek. And once it had been freed, the others followed before she could stop them. She walked, crying without a sound, not wiping her face, just letting the tears drip from her jaw, the tip of her chin, letting her nose run, letting whatever clung to her chest cling tighter, harder, with barbs like thorns, until she sagged against a tree in the middle of a block and covered her face with her arms. The whip dangled between her fingers. The bark scratched her spine. Her legs bent until she settled on a great knee of a root, pulled her own knees up and pressed her eyes into them until there were sparks and pinwheels and a muffled, lonely sobbing.

Forever.

Nothing else.

"You hurt?"

Her head snapped up so sharply she yanked the muscles in her neck, and that made her angry. "No!" she said, rubbing her nape, burying a wince with a frown.

The girl in front of her leaned over, hands on her knees, blond pigtails—oh *god,* pigtails—flapping over her shoulders. "So how come you're crying?"

"I'm not," she insisted, getting the backs of her hands to work across her eyes, under her nose. "I got allergies, okay? That all right with you?"

The girl shrugged. T-shirt and shorts and sneakers without socks. "I don't care. I just thought you were hurt, that's all." She looked up and down the street. "So, you visiting or what?"

"I live here."

"No kidding?" Another look, this time searching. "Where?"

Fran waved her right hand. "That way, I think. I don't know. Someplace."

The girl seemed puzzled.

Fran didn't feel like helping.

"Oh. You're lost, huh. My name is Kitt."

Fran's disgusted look took care of the lost question but, as she pushed herself to her feet, she said, "Kitt?"

"Yeah. Kitt Weatherall. Kitt's short for kitten. That's what my father calls me." She glanced hopelessly at the sky. "Now everybody calls me that."

"Kitten?"

"No! Kitt. I don't want to be called kitten all my life. God."

A final swipe across her face. "My father calls me 'pal' sometimes."

"Ugh," Kitt said. "Like you were a boy or something."

"Yeah. Ugh."

They walked, and the day's heat cooled in the shifting speckled shade.

"So you're new?"

"Yeah. I guess."

"You going in sixth grade?"

Fran nodded.

"Me too."

They both aimed for a spider scurrying over the pavement, nearly stepped on each other's foot, and giggled.

"You got any brothers or anything?"

Fran used her whip to decapitate a low weed. "Nope."

"Me neither. If I had a brother, I'd probably kill him."

"Yeah, me too."

They reached a broad street, a large church on the corner, its greystone walls stained with faint green age. A steeple that didn't impress her with its height. A signboard in the shape of a crest near the entrance proclaimed it to be Anglican; Fran wasn't sure what that meant but didn't want to ask.

Kitt pointed to the left. "That way's Mainland Road. It's the only road to get here from wherever unless you take the train." To the right. "Up the Pike—this is Williamston Pike—there are some really neat houses. Monsters. I mean, people live out there who are richer than God."

Fran stared down toward the Road. She could see a blinking amber light and not much traffic. The only way out. What kind of a place was this that only had one way out?

She wasn't stuck; she was trapped.

"Hey," said Kitt, a quick touch, a drop of the hand. "It isn't that bad."

Fran shook her head quickly.

"No, really. I mean, it's not like we've got a zoo or Disneyland or anything, but there's the park and the pond, a whole bunch of ducks live there all summer, and we can ride horses out in the valley sometimes, and the woods and all and . . ." She wrinkled her face until Fran thought it would disappear. "And the Pilgrim's Travelers are here." She gestured vaguely. "On the other side of the Road."

"Travelers? What's that."

"It's a carnival thing, like a circus kind of. You know, rides and food and stuff. Sometimes they stay just for a little while, sometimes it's like they're around for practically the whole summer."

"Oh." No excitement, no anticipation. She could just imagine what a circus would be like in a dump like this, especially one that had no place else to go. "So that's it?"

Kitt shrugged. "Yeah, I guess. But it's better than living in the city, that's for sure."

"How would you know?" She felt heat in her cheeks and the heated tears gathering for another charge. "I lived in Cambridge. That's pretty neat."

Kitt wasn't impressed. "I used to live in New York, when I was a kid."

Fran glanced at the church again and thought about how old it must be to look that old. Like the fence in her backyard, it looked old enough to fall down any minute, yet the stones it was made of looked thick and big enough to last forever. She frowned. That wasn't right. How could something look weak and strong at the same time? That was dumb. She was dumb. This whole place was dumb.

"Shit," she said disgustedly.

Kitt's eyes widened.

Fran grinned. "Hey, I thought you lived in New York."

"Yeah, but I never said stuff like that." A half-trembling

smile. "I ever said something like that, god, my mother would wash my mouth out with soap, I'd be grounded for a year."

"Yeah, well—"

A faint whirring startled her. A brief metallic sputtering, and suddenly bells in the steeple clanged tunelessly, and so rapidly she didn't think to count them until Kitt said, "Nuts, it's five already."

Fran didn't believe it. It couldn't be. That meant she'd been walking all afternoon, walking all over and not once leaving town.

"Hey," said Kitt, "I gotta go. Maybe I'll see you tomorrow?"

"Sure," Fran said, still staring at the church, at the dark rectangles in the stone tower the bells hid behind.

Five o'clock?

Then Kitt faced her toward Mainland Road, gently. "Two blocks down that way, turn left, two blocks more. I know you're not lost, but that's where you live anyway." A grin that exposed a missing tooth on the bottom. "See you." And she ran in the opposite direction, dragging her shadow behind her until she rounded a corner and disappeared.

I don't like this place, Fran decided as she headed for the place where she lived now, it wasn't home; I don't like a place where people know where you live when you didn't even tell them.

But by the time she reached her front walk, she hated herself for already recognizing a few of the houses, for thinking they weren't all that bad, not really, some of them were actually kind of pretty in a weird sort of way. Different colors on one place. Red and cream; dark blue and white; grey and maroon. They were big enough that it kind of looked good. Not old, not like she first thought; at least not falling-down old.

Even the house where she lived now—two stories and lots of that stuff her mother called gingerbread, fresh white and dark green, and her room right over the front-porch roof on the left, she could tell from the curtains her mother had hung in the open window. They waved at her. Slowly. Reaching out and sighing, sliding back in. Suddenly she was mad enough to want to run in and tear them down from their rods, stamp all over them, drag them through mud and dirt and leave them in the street where cars would run over them; and just as suddenly it left her, and left her puffing as if she had run a million miles, making her so tired that she nearly had to crawl to the steps, sit down, elbows on knees, cheeks in palms.

Trapped.

"Fran?" Her mother calling from inside. "Fran, we're going to eat in a few minutes."

"Yeah, okay." She hunched her shoulders, made herself small, like the small brown bird with the touch of yellow on his head that sauntered across the grass like he owned it. He stabbed at something on the walk and moved on, popping into the bushes that separated her house from the one next door.

When she looked back to the street, someone was standing on the sidewalk.

She sat up abruptly; it was a boy. He wore a baseball shirt with the sleeves rolled up, baseball pants, and sneakers that had a black band around the edge. His hair was thick and brown, and streaked with light, as if he spent most of his day in the hot sun.

"Hi," he said, not shy at all.

She sort of smiled, keeping most of it in because she didn't want to act like a jerk, because he was, after all, only a boy even if he was cute.

He looked the house over. "You just moved in, I bet."

She nodded.

He kept one hand in a hip pocket. Any minute now she expected him to start chewing tobacco.

"Fran, supper!"

She grimaced.

"Fran." The boy worked his mouth around it like something he hadn't ever eaten before and wasn't sure how it tasted.

"Short for Frances," she told him brusquely, blinking rapidly because she didn't know she still had a voice, or could use it. "I hate Frances. I hate Fran too, but it's better than nothing."

He grinned, his cheeks fat like a chipmunk after a full meal. Then, to her embarrassment, he pointed at his cheeks, poked at them. "I'm Chip," he told her. "Because I look like a chipmunk."

"Who says that?"

"Everybody. You don't think so?"

"I don't know, turn around, I'll see if you have a stripe and a tail."

He laughed. "All right, Fran! Hey, you got a last name?"

Suspicious, she frowned. "What for?"

"So I can look you up in the phone book, dope, and call you sometime."

Maybe, she thought at him, I don't want you to call me, you ever think of that? Why would I want anyone called Chip to call me? Especially a boy.

"Lumbaird," she answered.

He nodded. "Okay. Mine's Clelland."

She shrugged *so?*

He straightened, his face without expression, and she wanted to fall under the steps, under the porch, hide there until the spiders got her.

"Fran?"

She turned quickly. "Mom, c'mon, just a few more minutes, okay?"

"It's ready," her mother said sternly from the other side of the screen door. Hardly seen. Only a pale glow from the skin on her arms and face. "And it's getting cold."

"Oh . . . all right."

She looked back to tell Chip . . . something, she didn't know what . . . but the sidewalk was empty. She scrambled to her feet and looked up and down the block, but no one was there. No one. He was gone. Only the trees. Still frowning, she wanted to run down the walk and check behind the bushes there because that's where he had to be. Hiding. He couldn't have run that far that fast just when she was talking to her mother.

"Frances. Now."

She stared; she couldn't see him.

She heard the door open and took the steps slowly.

Her mother guided her into the kitchen, to the sink and the soap. "Did you have a good walk, honey? Did you meet anyone?"

She told her about Kitt, about how the girl knew where she lived.

"Honey, in a town this small everyone knows everyone and where everyone lives."

Great.

"And I met a boy named Chip," she added as she dried her hands on paper towels.

"Oh, really?"

"Yep." She looked up at her mother and ignited her best smile. "I think he's a ghost."

* * *

The storm woke her.

She had been listening to it all day, grumbling like an old man off in the distance, stomping around the hills as if he couldn't make up his mind which way to go. Dark clouds and once in a while a gust of wind that picked up dust and blew it into the house, snapped the shades, snapped the curtains, fluttered the fringe on the living room carpet. Then calm. Not quiet, just still. The old man, out of breath, waiting for his strength to return. A peculiar smell that Daddy said meant rain was on the way. A tickling along her arms once in a while that Mom told her was lightning getting ready to strike.

They had been working for what felt like forever, putting the last things away, cleaning floors and windows, moving furniture to get the rugs down, moving the furniture back, taking breaks to get into the car and drive around the Station. Exploring. Finding a park that was huge, almost like another country even though they only stayed on the paths; eating in places called the Inn and the Cove and the Cock's Crow; seeing the movie theater that didn't look like one she ever saw but at least it gave her hope; looking at her new school on High Street that made her depressed because it was stone and something else old even though it was right near the park entrance; seeing the library, a sort of modern building that she knew right away just didn't belong. Once, driving across the railroad tracks and into the valley where she saw the farms and a quarry and Pilgrim Creek and she wanted to scream because there wasn't anything out there but grass and crops and a couple of cows that didn't even bother to look up when they drove by.

Then working again, and eating, and sleeping, and working because her parents said they wanted it all out of the way before the real summer began and it was too hot.

The storm woke her.

She hadn't even had time to find Kitt or Chip, and neither of them had stopped by, though a couple of other kids had— Elly Gulsing and Susan Dumont, who looked like sisters but weren't, and who spent that first hour telling her about the school and the teachers and the boys and stuff. Elly, who for god's sake wore a dress and sounded like she owned everything but the churches, said there was always something going on at the park pond, Fran ought to come over as soon as she was allowed; Susan, who dressed normally and had enormous dimples and was heavier but not really fat, said you can get ice cream and stuff at stands in the park, sometimes they spend all day there if they have enough money for a hot dog lunch. Fran said it sounded great, but she couldn't imagine spending a whole day, wasting all that daylight, sitting around watching ducks and talking and making plans to take over the world. Boring. It sounded boring.

They came by a couple of times, alone or together, talked, left, and left behind bits of themselves that Fran passed on to her parents—like Elly's father being some sort of banker in Boston, like Susan being a twin but her sister had died of cancer two years ago, like Kitt's father owning the delicatessen on High Street and letting his daughter's friends swipe some summer fruit now and then.

The storm woke her.

Then a man came by, Mr. Chase from the hardware store, with a station wagon filled with kids. He knew Daddy and wanted to know if they wanted to go to the Travelers with him. Mom didn't think so, Daddy said there was still a ton of things to do around the house, but before Fran could protest, they made a miracle happen—they let her go without them, with a promise to listen to Mr. Chase and not go off on her own.

A miracle.

She almost cried.

And before she could think, the air smelled of sawdust and spun sugar, mustard and hamburgers, grease and machines. Elly was there, and Susan, and Kitt, and time passed in a gulp of soda, a smear of mustard licked off her thumb, and suddenly Mr. Chase said time for one more ride.

She picked the carousel, picked an ostrich, and prayed that the bird would jump off the platform and run her home. A hundred times in a circle, a million times, laughing, almost forgetting how miserable she was when she saw Chip on a stallion a few rows ahead. She called. He didn't hear her. He was talking to a skinny girl with straight hair riding beside him. Fran called again. He looked over his shoulder, stared, grinned recognition, waved, but the music was too loud for her to hear what he said when he tried to call back.

After the ride, feeling dizzy, she tried to find him, but Mr. Chase was waiting at the exit to take them all home.

The storm woke her.

A sound like slow-ripping metal sat her up abruptly, clutching the sheet to her chest; an enormous explosion of thunder and the storm wasn't an old man anymore, it was a bull running wild. At first she was scared. Cambridge didn't have storms like this. Not with lightning that lasted forever and seared shadows into the walls; not with thunder that lasted forever, crashing, then echoing, and echoing again, the bull running away and turning around to charge one more time.

Kicking up pebbles of rain that bounced off the porch roof and smashed against her window.

But as it settled in, the thunder constant but not as loud,

the lightning fierce but not as hot, the house no longer vibrating, she scolded herself for acting like a baby. A calming count to seven. She left her bed, padded to the window, squinting against the bright flares, scratching her sides, through her hair, leaning close enough to the pane for her breath to make a cloud she wiped away with the heel of her hand.

Lightning, this time silent, and the houses across the street were without color; lightning, silent, and the rain in the street was silver fire and silver sparks; lightning, and someone stood under the branches of the tree at the foot of her new driveway.

She almost didn't see him.

A dark figure that blended in with the bole, and it took two more strikes before she knew he was really there.

Chip?

No; it must be after midnight.

It was too dark in spite of all the light, and he was too far away from the nearest streetlamp to be seen without the lightning. But he stood there nevertheless, a shadow beside a shadow, not moving even though the wind slanted the rain and turned the street to a river of deep black ice.

He stood there; she could see him.

What a jerk, she thought; she wasn't afraid, just curious why his parents would let him out so late. Unless, she thought with a grin, he had snuck out. In the storm. Which instantly made her want to know why.

To see you, stupid.

Oh sure, tell me another one.

Really, I'm not kidding.

Quickly she grabbed up her bathrobe and ran out of the room, keeping on her toes even though the wind had found a voice to howl with and moan. This afternoon the stairs had been carpeted, the last thing done before Mom declared the moving officially over, and she hurried down, not really sure she wouldn't slip in the soft pile, ran into the living room and pulled aside the drapery, and the shade.

Waited.

Only a few droplets quivered on the glass here, the porch roof keeping most of the rain away, and when the lightning came again, distant, wan, almost weary of the game, she pressed her forehead against the cold pane and couldn't see him no matter how hard she stared. She bit down on her lower lip gently, pulled at it with her teeth. Another bolt, and she couldn't be sure.

"Damn," she whispered, moved into the foyer and checked the staircase to be sure no one else was awake and prowling around. Then she opened the front door, and shivered as cold and damp swirled hungrily around her ankles, burrowed into the skin on calf and shin, tightened the planes of her stomach and buttocks.

She still couldn't see him.

Thunder, loud and stomping away.

A second check of the staircase. She opened the screen door and, with a deep breath, stepped onto the porch, hugging herself when the storm cold leaped out of the shrubs and grabbed her, telling herself she was a jerk, a dope, a real first-class idiot, she was going to catch pneumonia and her father would kill her.

This time she saw him.

Without the lightning. When her vision adjusted. When the rain, just for a second, was split by the wind, she saw him standing by the tree, one arm around the bole as if to keep himself from being blown away. He was dressed the way she had first seen him, but she frowned when she realized that he wasn't touched by the storm—his hair wasn't flying, his clothes weren't wet.

She wondered if she should wave, let him know she had seen him.

"Looking for your ghost?"

She screamed and froze, became rigid when hands took her shoulders and lifted her, held her, and a voice whispered *god, I'm sorry* over and over again, turned her around away from the wind and she could see over her father's shoulder and could see that Chip was gone. Her teeth began to chatter. She bit her tongue, yelped, and he took her inside, straight to the kitchen, sat her at the table and turned on the light over the stove. A small light. Just enough for her to see him, but not his eyes.

Without speaking he warmed some milk in a pan, poured her a small glass, poured himself one and sat.

"Nightmare?" A soft question.

The old man, the bull, was gone, leaving the rain behind to rattle across the roof and splash out of the gutters.

She hated warm milk, it was for little kids and old people, but it tasted good when she sipped it.

"No. The thunder woke me."

"It always sounds louder with all these hills around, all this open space." He chuckled. "They're no worse than the ones back in Cambridge, they just sound that way." He pointed at the ceiling. "It woke me too. Your mother, on the other hand, that woman will sleep through World War III."

She nodded.

"So, what were you doing on the porch?"

A shrug.

A yawn.

"Fran."

In the dim light she could see a smile, gentle.

"I know it's been hard, really I do. But we're all done now, and you can meet some more kids, have a good time the rest of the summer. I just . . . I didn't realize how much work it would be, and I'm sorry. Must be kind of lonely, huh?"

A shrug.

A wider yawn.

The milk had cooled; she pushed the glass away.

He stood, and held out his arms. "C'mon."

She was too old and they both knew it, but to make him happy she let him pick her up, let her chin rest on his shoulder while he turned off the light just as the old man returned, turned into the bull, and slammed the house with a jolt that startled them both. Her father laughed. She snuggled closer, hands tucked against her neck as they moved down the hall and started up the stairs.

She yawned so hard her jaw popped, and she giggled, felt her eyes begin to close and was glad they did because if they hadn't, if she had been wide awake, she would have had to tell her father that Chip was standing on the porch.

Fever dream.

Hot and cold monsters fighting in her blood.

Hot hands and cold hands pressed tenderly against her cheeks, brushing damp hair from her brow, settling a thin blanket beneath her chin.

Chip walking through the wall to say hi. Checking out the room. Telling her it was nice. Waving good-bye when the sun went down.

Blood on the inside of her cheek when she bit it.

Warm hands.

Cool hands.

"I just don't understand it."

"For crying out loud, Lanette, how many times do I have to say I'm sorry? I didn't realize she was that wet. She wasn't outside that long. And she was fine when I put her to bed."

"She was on the porch, for god's sake, in the middle of a storm, and all you gave her is a glass of milk. You didn't even dry her off. She's lucky she isn't in a hospital."

"Good lord, the doctor said it's only a cold. She's had colds before. Dozens of them. It isn't going to kill her."

"I hate this place. God, I hate this place."

"Now you're being silly."

"Me? Silly? Who's the one who said construction in a place like this was going to make us rich? Who gave up a perfectly good partnership and threw in with people he didn't even know?"

"Lanette—"

"Have you looked around lately, Neal? Have you seen how many new houses are going up? I didn't see a goddamn one! Even the houses that aren't a hundred years old look it, for Christ's sake."

"Oh, right, like I kidnapped you, huh? Like I dragged you and the kid to the middle of nowhere, kicking and screaming."

"Well it is nowhere, Neal. And it's in the middle of no-where."

"Don't be stupid."

"Go to hell."

"Jesus Christ, all this for just a goddamn cold? What the hell are you going to be like when she breaks a leg or some-thing?"

"Don't say that. Don't you *ever* say that."

Fever dream.

Hands.

Ostrich taking her away, a boy effortlessly racing beside her.

"Who's Chip?"

"I don't know. One of those kids, I guess. I don't remember."

"Sounds like a boy."

"So what? She knows boys, you know, Neal. It's not like she's never seen one before."

"Why didn't she tell us about him?"

"Hush, she's sleeping."

"I didn't know she had a boyfriend."

"I'm sure she doesn't have a boyfriend already, Neal. Lord. You sound just like a father."

"I'm just curious. She talks about that Kitt girl and those other kids—I just wonder why she never told us about this Chip."

"Maybe it's because you never give her a chance. You've got her working like a slave around here."

"Jesus, not that again."

"Keep your voice down."

"I just want to know about this boy, that's all. What are you trying to do, hang me for asking?"

"Well, why don't you just shake it out of her, huh? Big man. Ask her if she's sleeping with him, why not."

"That's disgusting."

"See? Big man. Just leave us alone, Neal. Go back to your goddamn grass and your goddamn bushes and goddamn leave us alone."

Fever dream.

*   *   *

On Sunday morning Fran marched into the kitchen and told her father that if she didn't go someplace else besides the front porch or the backyard right away she was going to throw a tantrum, hold her breath until her face turned blue, scream until her head fell off, break every piece of furniture in the house, have a heart attack and die.

He picked her up and they glared at each other. She could feel his arms trembling with her weight.

"Bored, huh?"

"I'm dying!"

"You look pretty good to me."

"I'm dying, Daddy."

"You've been sick."

"That was days ago!"

Nose touched nose, and she felt her eyes want to cross, her lips want to smile.

"How about a walk?"

"More than just around the block."

"The carnival?"

"It's not open during the day. Kitt told me."

"Okay, the park?"

She nodded.

He put her down, aimed an open hand at her head which she ducked and ran out of the kitchen, grinning, catching her mother by the arm as Lanette walked out of the living room, telling her they were going over the wall, not to alert the warden or the bulls will shoot them down in cold blood and burn their bodies with the trash.

"Where on earth did you hear that?"

Fran shrugged. "TV, I guess." She took her mother's hand and tugged it, gently. "C'mon, we're going to the park."

"We?"

"All of us," Neal agreed, joining them in the foyer, rubbing his palms together. "Cabin fever is my diagnosis. Best cure in the world is some ice cream, junk food, and a walk under the trees."

Lanette shook her head. "I don't think so. It must be a hundred out there."

"Eighty-eight," Fran told her. A shrug at her expression. "I heard it on the radio." She tugged again. "C'mon, Mom, please? It's not that hot." Nothing; only a glance at her father. "I promise I won't run around, okay? I'll sit. I'll lie down." She let her lower lip tremble. "Mom, c'mon."

It was like the storm again before it struck—electricity she could feel, thunder she could hear like the rush of blood in her ear. Daddy called it cabin fever; she called it wanting to get out before somebody killed somebody. All that silence made her nervous.

The knock on the screen door, then, made her jump, made her mother slip back into the living room, as if sliding into a closet.

It was Kitt, and someone else.

"Hi," Fran said, too loudly.

Kitt grinned. "Wanna go to the park? This is Drake Saxton. He lives in my neighborhood, next door, really." The smile slipped to a curled lip of disdain. "He's gonna baby-sit us. Mom's paying him,"

He was tall, thin, had ten times as much hair as her father, and Fran couldn't believe they actually needed a baby-sitter in the middle of the day practically.

"Hey," Drake said.

Fran didn't think he was all that thrilled either.

Neal introduced himself, and Fran slipped onto the porch

to stand beside Kitt while Drake told Fran's father that he was playing ball with his buddies today and had promised Mrs. Weatherall he'd look after Kitt. Fran could tell he hated it, even if he was getting money for it; she could tell her father didn't care that Drake hated it when he said after a glance over his shoulder, "Maybe I'll stay home, then, work in the garden. You sure you don't mind, son?"

Of course he does, Fran answered with a disgusted look, but Drake only shrugged a *makes no never mind to me one way or the other*.

"You be good," Neal cautioned.

Fran rolled her eyes. Kitt giggled, grabbed her hand, and they ran down the steps.

"Hey!"

They stopped.

"Fran, home by supper."

She nodded, waved, waved to her mother standing at the window, and they ran again, not caring whether Drake caught up with them or not, not slowing until they reached High Street and turned east where the heat at last reached them, and the sweat broke free on their backs and brows. Kitt said they should have brought their bathing suits, some of the others probably had, but Fran didn't answer with more than a grunt. She was free, that's what mattered; she was out of the house, away from the looks and the snide remarks and the way her parents avoided each other and didn't think she noticed. Ever since the storm. Ever since Daddy had said something at dinner about all the work he couldn't find, times were tough, it wasn't his fault. She would have gone out naked if that's the way it had to be.

She glanced over her shoulder. "He doesn't like you or what?" she said.

Kitt, chewing on the end of a pigtail, waved a hand. "He's too good for us. Big man. Just like my brother."

"Oh." Another glance. He was a block behind, catching up without running, staring at his sneakers. "I thought you said you didn't have a brother?"

"He's not my real brother. The Martians brought him one night when I wasn't looking. Drake came with him, in the garbage bag."

Fran laughed.

Kitt punched her arm lightly.

"They're in high school, huh, your brother and him?"

Kitt made a face. "No. Junior's in college. Ricky—he's my Martian brother—he wants to be an actor, can you believe it? Make movies and plays and stuff. Big deal. At least *he* thinks he is." She covered her mouth and laughed. "I saw him kissing a girl last night. God, it was gross."

"I'll bet," Fran agreed. Lips touching lips. Mom and Daddy. "Ugh. So where are we going?"

"The pond. Elly says it's time you got a friend around here."

Fran stared. "Aren't you my friend?"

"Well, yeah, but this is different."

"What do you mean?"

Kitt pushed her playfully. "You'll see. It's a secret."

"I hate secrets."

"Me too." She laughed again.

By the time they reached Centre Street, the shops and offices closed, no one on the sidewalks, Drake was right behind them, baseball bat over one shoulder, baseball cap pulled down and sullen over his eyes.

"You don't have to follow us, you know," Kitt told him

without turning around. "You're not a shadow, in case you hadn't noticed."

"Don't be a pain, Kitt," he answered glumly. "And I'm not gonna follow you, okay? I got better things to do."

"Just see that you don't."

Fran said nothing. She didn't know if this was the way you were supposed to talk to friends of big brothers, so she let Kitt do it all. And she did. All the way to the park. Telling him not to spoil her fun, stay a hundred miles away and leave her friends alone or she'd tell his mother what she saw him doing in his car the week before. A giggle. Fran hated that sound. Kitt made it like she couldn't breathe right and had to gargle when she did. It was ugly.

They passed the tobacco shop, piles of Sunday papers stacked by the door, and the delicatessen where Kitt wondered aloud why Drake wasn't behind the counter helping her father if he really wanted to make some money, and the hardware store locked up and dark in spite of the sun. Across Park Street, then, and Fran looked at the high iron fencing that fronted the park, at the open iron gates through which people strolled now, pushing carriages, carrying baseball gloves and picnic baskets, kids running despite the weather; into the shade made by trees so close together, so high, so thick around, she thought she had fallen back into her dream, fever dream, and she had to shake her head to clear it, and trot to catch up with Kitt, who had swerved to the right and was making her way along a worn path between shrubs that had big shiny leaves but no flowers.

Jungle.

Like the backyard.

Until they reached the other side and she stopped, gaping.

"Wow," she said quietly.

A huge expanse of grass right in front of her, tall ever-greens on the far side; to the left a ballfield, and beyond it a large white bandstand at the foot of a hill that sloped gently upward to more trees on top. It was like the country in the middle of a city, she thought; riding past it in the car had given her no idea that it looked like this.

"Neat, huh?" Kitt said, grinning.

She nodded.

Drake leaned over, bat in both hands, and looked at Kitt. "You going to the pond?"

"The moon."

"Suits me," he said. "Just don't leave without me, okay? You do, I'll pound you."

"Oh boy, I'm so scared."

He looked at Fran, and suddenly smiled so broadly she couldn't help but smile back. "When you're ready to go home, lady, I'll be right here, all right? Don't let her talk you into anything stupid."

"Sure," she said.

"Sure," Kitt echoed sarcastically, and bolted across the grass. "C'mon, Lumbaird, leave the creep to the creeps!"

Fran ran.

Around people on sheets and blankets sunning themselves, burning themselves, playing catch and slow tag and just walk-ing without having any real place to go; looking over once to see Drake joining his friends, pushing and shoving and threat-ening with the bat; looking to the right to the spear-tips of the fence that rose above the shrubs and between the trees, but not being able to see the village on the other side; breaking through the evergreens behind Kitt. And stopping again.

"Damn," she whispered.

The pond was a bloated L shape, its high banks covered

with pine needles, the water a darker blue than the sky. Darker, almost black. A small rowboat anchored in the center, two people in it beneath a large umbrella. Another world again, a world within a world, and she wondered how many more surprises this place had.

She followed Kitt along the lip of the bank until they reached the far end. She knew Chancellor Avenue was out there, but the greenery cut it off, smothered the traffic's noise, and smothered the heat as well, making her shiver as she ducked under the branch of a multitrunk elm and found herself in a small glade whose grass had long since been trained to grow in ragged patches amid patches of dark earth where violets grew low. High, crisscrossed branches masked most of the sky, sliced the sun into fragments that barely lit the ground. Not quite twilight, not quite an autumn afternoon.

Elly was there, sitting primly on a folded tartan blanket, and Susan with her dimples, and two others she didn't recognize. Kitt introduced them, but Fran couldn't hold onto their names right away, and maybe didn't want to the way they looked at her. Sideways, not straight on, checking her out, measuring her. Not really friendly. City kid. She found a place to sit—behind and to the right of Elly, on a root like the one where she'd cried on the day she'd arrived.

There were no boys.

Elly crossed her legs, smoothed her skirt with both hands, brushed her bangs carefully away from her eyes. "All right," she said, and the others quickly formed a ragged half circle in front of her. One of them—Maddy? she couldn't remember— glared at Fran until she deliberately looked away. She wasn't about to play this game until she knew the rules. All of them. And being like some kind of servant to some kind of queen wasn't what Daddy would call her style.

Elly didn't seem to mind.

The faint *crack* of bat and ball.

A duck calling to another, was answered, and calling again.

A bumblebee checking the flowers, Fran watching it uneasily, praying it wouldn't come near though she could hear it buzzing loud and soft, loud and soft, swaying side to side in the air and moving on, and buzzing.

Then Kitt said, "Fran hasn't got a friend."

Maddy—was it Maddy? Maggie? who cared, she was fat and had frizzy hair—looked at her sorrowfully, and Fran felt her temper tug a scowl into place. What was going on here? She had a friend. Kitt was one. Maybe Elly, maybe Susan. That was three. She had lots of friends back in Cambridge. Tons of them. What was going on?

Elly nodded, and brushed at her skirt. "She's been here long enough, but does she want one?"

Kitt chewed on the end of a pigtail, lifted one shoulder.

"Hey," Fran said.

They all looked at her. Except Elly.

"I'm here, you know," she said, pointing at her chest. "It's not like I'm a ghost or anything. Why don't you just ask me?"

Elly swiveled around, smoothed her skirt, brushed at her bangs. Smiled sweetly. "Do you?"

"Do I what?"

"Want a friend."

"I've got them."

Maddy laughed, and cut herself off.

"What is this, some kind of club?" Fran shook her head, not liking the way they were so serious. "You guys some kind of club?" She looked at Kitt. "What?"

Kitt pulled the end of her pigtail out of her mouth and

plucked at the grass beside her. It wasn't a club, she said, not exactly. It was kind of like some of the kids hung out, that's all, and when one of them got in trouble, the others kind of helped out, stuff like that. Homework, teachers, brothers, stuff like that. Finding things that got lost, chipping in when you couldn't afford a new necklace or headband or wristband, stuff like that. Sometimes, when you needed a friend, they kind of helped out there too, checking the guy out, making sure he was all right, wasn't a creep, a dork, a scuzzbag, stuff like that. Sometimes you couldn't tell. Sometimes they smiled at you, said things to you, you think maybe he likes you, but he really doesn't, he just wants to pretend like he's something else, not just a kid with zits and glop.

"A boyfriend?" Fran said, not believing what she'd heard. "You . . ." She laughed, but not aloud.

New kids didn't know about the kids who already lived here, Kitt went on. New kids sometimes got hurt when they didn't have to be hurt, didn't have to cry themselves to sleep every night, didn't have to make a jackass of herself over some jerk who couldn't even remember her stupid telephone number. The old kids helped the new kids. Stuff like that.

Fran didn't know whether to laugh, get mad, tell them they were nuts, tell them without knowing why she wanted to that her parents had started to fight every night when they thought she was asleep, could they help her with that with their stupid little club? But she didn't say anything. Because the expressions they had weren't hostile any longer, or uncaring, or suspicious; they were patient. As if they had read her thoughts, or had had them before themselves, and were just waiting for her to make up her mind that things were really okay, there wasn't anything she had to worry about. Not here.

It almost made her cry.

"There's this kid who came around once," she said at last, and shook her head. "Twice. I saw him at the carnival too."

They waited.

"Chip. He said his name is Chip."

"Chip Clelland?" Elly said as if she hadn't heard the name correctly.

Fran nodded.

"You want him for a friend?"

She shrugged. "I don't know. He's nice, I guess. Not a boy-friend. He doesn't have to be a boyfriend, does he?"

"Hell, no," said Maddy as she unwrapped a chocolate bar, her offer to share untaken. "Besides, boys are dumb shits any-way."

Kitt and Susan giggled.

"Language," Elly said softly.

Maddy stuck out her tongue.

"Mine," a voice said then. Frail. Quiet; so quiet it screamed.

Fran looked around, wondering who else had joined them, and saw the fifth girl staring at her. Pale, scrawny, her T-shirt baggy though it couldn't get much smaller; her legs were crossed, the flesh stretched so tightly across her knees, the white of the bone showed through. Her elbows were the same.

Fran recognized her then—the girl on the carousel, the one riding with, talking to, laughing with Chip.

"Mine," she repeated, from behind limp bangs that nearly covered her eyes.

Maddy snorted, jabbing an elbow into Susan's ribs; Susan slapped the arm away, but Fran saw that she was grinning.

"We know that, Zera," Elly snapped. "You don't have to

keep telling us all the time." She rolled her eyes, plucked at her skirt. "The problem is—"

"Tell her," Zera persisted. She looked at Fran without expression. "Tell her."

"Oh for god's sake," Maddy said, and squinted up at the sky. "Look, we gonna be here all day or what? I'm going shopping with my mom in Harley."

"So go," Susan said.

Maddy didn't move.

The bumblebee landed on the root between Fran's legs, and she watched it turning in a slow confused circle, almost didn't hear Elly tell her that Chip was Zera's friend, and you didn't share friends, that's not the way it worked, but if Fran really wanted one they would see what they could do even if she was new. Susan said it was too hot, that she was going to fry, that she wanted to wade in the pond, and if all they were going to do was sit around and bitch, then she was leaving.

"So go," Maddy said with a smirk.

Susan didn't move.

Fran looked up; they were watching her. Waiting. When she glanced back at the root, the bee was gone.

"Well?" Elly asked impatiently.

"Well what?" Fran pushed herself to her feet, dusted off her backside. This was no fun, no fun at all; if she'd wanted to listen to people talk like this, she could've stayed home.

"Do you want one or not?"

It was almost a command.

Fran bridled. "If I want a friend, I'll get my own, okay?" She shook her head. "You guys are nuts, you know that?"

A quick disgusted wave to Kitt, and she walked around the tree, into the bushes. Angry at herself for getting angry at something so stupid. Angry at them for as much as telling her she couldn't see Chip because he was Zera's friend. What kind of a friend was that, that you only belonged to one person? And what kind of a name was Zera anyway?

She slapped a branch aside and came out on the pond's east bank. The ducks were still there, the rowboat gone, and she walked slowly, every few paces picking up a pebble and tossing it sideways into the water. Watching the splash. Watching the ripples die before they reached the shore. Sunlight caught and shattered on the surface.

Beyond the evergreens she paused, indecisive, then swung to her right and walked along the field's edge. Kicking at the grass. Watching the sunbathers. Listening to low music from radios set on the ground. Watching the ball game and answering a wave from Drake in the outfield. Passing another open stretch with the bandstand on the far side.

Climbing the low hill.

Where she sat when she reached the top, and looked out, looked down.

She hated this place.

Kids that started out okay and ended up as snotty as the kids she knew back home, the ones who snickered at her and teased her because she wasn't quite as fast, quite as strong, quite as smart, quite as anything as anybody else. She knew the words and she knew the moves, but somehow they had never quite all fit together. She wasn't the only one. She knew that. But it didn't make it feel any better. And here, she could tell they didn't think she fit either. Maddy, Elly, that weird Zera . . . they didn't know it, any of them, but they were a club that had dumb rules just like all clubs had, and the way they talked to and about Elly made her the queen of the club.

The Queen of the Club.

What a joke.

Someone sat beside her.

She moved her eyes, not her head, and saw Chip with his legs crossed, a shirt with the sleeves rolled above the elbows, jeans with patches and carefully torn holes. His feet were bare. He smelled, for a moment, like cotton candy.

"Hot," he said, nodding toward the field.

"Yeah."

"Hot up here too, but at least there's a breeze."

"Yeah."

She could feel him looking at her, and it made her feel funny.

He poked her thigh with a knuckle. "Been with the jerks, huh?"

"How did you know?" Still not looking.

"You look like you want to kill somebody."

A hesitation before she nodded.

"Bet Zera told you to keep your hands off me, I'm hers, private property, keep out, no trespassing, right?"

Fran almost laughed. She nodded instead.

"You gonna let them boss you around?"

She did look this time. He smiled. She smiled back. "Not me. I told them to go jump."

"That's good." He picked up a pebble, flicked it away. "You let them boss you around like they were your mother or something, they'll do it in school too, they'll even do it in high school, you'll end up so miserable you'll want to kill yourself." He watched the game for a while. "You know Susan? Dumont?"

"Yes. Her sister died or something."

"I know," he said quietly. "She was a friend of mine. For a long time."

Fran didn't know what to say, followed a crow instead that chased a dozen sparrows away from something in the grass.

"You know, Fran, there are other kids to hang out with around here. Not a lot, but others."

"You gonna be my friend?" she asked before she could think.

His head swiveled toward her slowly.

Bat and ball; children yelling.

"You mean that?"

A shrug, a nod, a shrug again. "Yeah, I guess so. Yeah."

She stared then at his profile, saw skin jump as muscles twitched, saw what might have been a grin pull back the corner of his mouth.

"Maybe," he said at last.

Her scowl didn't make him turn, and she looked back at the game, where Drake had just dropped a fly ball. "Maybe? What do you mean, maybe? I gotta do something first, huh? Some kind of test?"

"Not you," he answered. "Me."

"Well, forget it," she said angrily. "You don't have to take a test to be a friend, y'know. Not where I came from, anyway. That's stupid. Is that the way they do it here? God. That's so dumb I can't believe it."

He didn't answer.

She grabbed a clump of grass and yanked it out, threw it down the slope.

"I don't pass any tests," she muttered.

It didn't matter.

He was gone.

She didn't wait for Drake; she started home alone, sometimes praying that Kitt would show up so she could ignore her, sometimes hoping she'd meet her father along the way so he could take her someplace for an ice cream.

A man was cleaning the hardware-store window as she passed, the sidewalk dark with splashed water. She knew him. Mayard Chase. Besides taking her to the Travelers, he'd come to the house a couple of other times to talk with her father about building and stuff. He wasn't very tall, but he was big. Muscle big. And not much hair except for a red fringe above his ears.

He smiled at her.

She smiled back.

"You settling in?" he asked.

"I guess."

"Pain in the neck, isn't it?"

She slowed, watching him hunker down to scrub a low corner of the glass. "What is?"

"Trying to decide if you want to stick around or run away."

An automatic protest choked her, and all she could do was shake her head.

He rose with a loud groan, a hand on his lower back. He stepped back to the curb and examined the window. "What do you think?"

She looked. "It's clean, I guess."

"Yeah." He nodded, hands on his hips now. "Nobody ever notices when it's clean, you know. Only when it's dirty." A laugh just shy of being too high-pitched. "I've got three boys and two girls, and they don't even know it's there at all." Another laugh, deep in his throat. "Tell your dad I said hello, okay? I'll call him this week."

She nodded, and headed for the corner. As she crossed the empty street she looked back, and he was back down again, scrubbing at the corner. Weird, she thought, and giggled when she realized that Mr. Chase fit. If the place was weird, and Mr. Chase was weird, then they belonged here.

God, she hoped she'd never get weird.

The house was empty when she got there.

She didn't have to call out; she could feel it.

The car was gone from the driveway, the garage was empty.

In a brief panic she ran up the stairs and checked the bedrooms just to be sure they hadn't changed their minds and went back home without her. But all the clothes were there, the beds unmade, and there was the smell of her mother's soap in the bathroom, the kind she used when she took a shower. So she took a can of soda from the refrigerator and sat on the porch railing, not caring how the sweat rolled in iceballs down her spine, how the soda almost gave her a cramp. She sat for over an hour, listening to how the Station sounded.

Quiet.

Dead.

Until she realized that she'd been listening for those blaring horns and screaming kids and shrieking brakes and sirens calling and doors slamming and airplane engines rumbling overhead.

She blinked.

And it wasn't quiet after all.

Leaves moved, air moved, birds and insects and dogs and things she didn't know about yet but would.

She leaned back against a post, one leg up, and scratched her nose.

Actually, it wasn't all that bad. Not too terrible. Not as if she would kill herself or anything. Mr. Chase was pretty okay, the postman who wore a hat the way they did in the jungle was cranky-funny and, like Chip had said, there were other kids. Elly may be Queen of the Club, but she wasn't queen of everything. She grinned, took a drink. Maybe *she* would get to be queen of something. Have her own kingdom, boss all the peasants, tell Elly to take her dress and stick it where the sun don't shine.

And there wouldn't be any rules about how to have a friend.

The storm woke her.

It had been muggy all evening, and she had heard, just after supper, the old man stomping around the valley again. Not as angrily this time. Just cranky, that's all—stomping and muttering and once in a while whacking a hill with his cane to get out the lightning.

She told her mother about the Queen of the Club, angry, and hurt, and finally hating them aloud. Her mother had laughed at first at the rules and the way Fran described how the girls listened to Elly; then she sobered and told her that grown-ups are that way too, and sometimes you joined and sometimes you didn't. It didn't help. Fran already knew about grown-ups. What she wanted to know was if she should be friends with Chip anyway, even if the others didn't like it.

Do you like him, Lanette asked.

Yeah. Sure. He's okay. He's funny.

Then why should you let someone else tell you what friends you can have and what friends you can't?

The storm woke her.

Daddy spent most of the day in the backyard, beating the grass down, cutting it, hauling it away in plastic bags to the curb. Cursing. Sometimes yelling. It wasn't like him at all, and for a while Fran thought Elly had snuck in one night and exchanged him for someone else. Someone Elly could add to the club and boss around.

When she told him about talking to Mr. Chase the day before, he only grunted and wished amid curses that the guy would mind his own damn business.

The storm woke her, and she sat up, rubbed her arms, knocked her hair away from her eyes; she hurried to the window and leaned against the sill, blinking against the flaring blue-white.

Looking for the lights of the carnival over the houses.

Looking for Chip.

Thunder, and lightning, but this time it was the wind that had all the fury, branches scraping against the house as if the trees wanted to get in, the rain on a hard slant, the house itself moaning, shifting, trembling, letting bits of the wind inside to keep the temperature down.

A throat cleared behind her.

She turned and saw her mother in the doorway, a ghost in a white nightgown, her hair loose and falling over her chest. She came in while Fran stared, swallowed, and looked outside again.

Lanette knelt on the floor, put her elbows on the sill. "It woke me up," she whispered, pointing to the rain that suddenly slashed against the window. "Are you all right, honey?"

"Yeah."

Shadows jumped—one second here, the next second over there.

"Mom, are you and Daddy going to get divorced?"

Lightning; she saw their faces in the pane, pale and long and twins.

"No, honey, I don't think so."

"Then why are you fighting all the time?"

A sigh the wind took and turned into a groan.

"It's not your daddy's fault. He was supposed to get a better position at the firm than he was promised, that's all." A hand on Fran's arm, a quick squeeze and it was gone. "It took about all we had to get here, move, fix the place, things like that. I don't like it when we don't have something in the bank." She smiled; it was killed by the lightning. "I get scared and I take it out on him sometimes."

Fran shivered. "Are we poor?"

"No, dear, we're not poor. It's what's called being a little tight for a while."

Shadow by the tree.

Fran squinted and strained.

"I'm sorry if we hurt you."

The storm, for a moment, gave the shadow a grinning face.

"It's okay."

Her mother kissed her cheek, hugged her shoulders, gently hustled her back to bed and kissed her again and whispered, "Everything's going to be all right, don't you worry."

"Okay."

Her mother hesitated. "Look, honey, I know it gets lonely when you don't have many friends. I'll find some. So will you. Get some sleep, now. See you in the morning."

Which came, and went.

As did the rest of the week, and the week after that.

She went to the park sometimes, all by herself because her mother got a job and wasn't home much anymore; once she went to the glade and found it empty, waited for a while and left. She watched ballgames and once in a while played with kids she didn't know who didn't ask her to play again unless she asked first. They didn't say no; they didn't invite her either.

She didn't see Chip.

She walked by Kitt's house a couple of times, saw Drake once, mowing his lawn, and he grinned and waved and called that Kitt was probably at the park. Fran couldn't find her.

One Saturday morning, all morning, her mother sat on the porch with red eyes and puffy cheeks and blew her nose a lot.

That night, they went to the carnival, but it wasn't much fun because her father kept saying how shoddy everything looked and her mother kept telling her to stay close, not to get lost, you never knew what kind of people worked at places like this.

Finally she managed to get them to the carousel.

"Oh, I couldn't," her mother said, shaking her head. "Neal, you know how I am. It'll make me sick."

Her father only frowned, but he let Fran go ahead and she raced on when it stopped, found her ostrich and grabbed the pole with both hands. On the first pass, her parents waved; they were gone the next time around, and the time after that, and she began to feel strange, a little scared, until Chip suddenly walked up beside her and put his hand on the bird's skinny neck.

She grinned.

He winked.

She said, "So, are we friends or what?"

"Soon," he told her, pinched her leg playfully as he darted away between the plunging animals.

Rules again, she thought; stupid dumb rules.

Three days later, Mr. Chase and two of his sons came over to visit, and they spent an hour on the porch, arguing with Daddy. Quietly, but she was up in her room and she could hear them anyway, and she finally decided to get out of the house so she couldn't hear anymore. Decided to find Chip, but he wasn't in the park, and the carnival was closed, and when she returned home, just before supper, her father was on the porch, reading the newspaper, and he said he was sorry about Zera Rainer.

Fran stared. "What?"

He beckoned, and she stood beside him, and saw on an inside page that Zera had died the night before in the hospital, from leukemia. He explained what it was, and said he was sorry again—wasn't she one of her friends? and she shrugged and went inside and stood in the middle of the living room and stared out the window, at the back of her father's head.

Waiting for the tears.

One finally came. Just one. Just as her mother came home, saw her, and hugged her, and asked her if she wanted to go to the funeral.

Fran shook her head.

Did she want to talk about it?

She shook her head again.

Waiting for the tears.

Going for a walk after a supper she knew she had eaten though she couldn't remember how it tasted, finding another branch-whip and dragging it behind her until she finally just let it drop.

In the park she started for the glade. They would be there. She knew it. But when she reached the trees she veered away and walked up the low hill, kicking the heads of grey-haired dandelions.

When she reached the top, she turned in a slow circle, sighed, and sat.

Waiting for the tears.

Chip came instead.

"Pretty bad, huh?" he said, grabbing at grass and tossing it into the air.

"Yeah."

He wore the same clothes, his feet were still bare.

"I didn't know," she said at last. "I didn't know she was so sick."

"She didn't either," he told her.

His voice made her look at him, made her frown because she couldn't understand how he could sound so . . . not uncaring . . . so normal. If Zera had been such a good friend, Fran would have been screaming her head off. She knew that. But Chip, from his eyes, hadn't been crying at all.

It scared her a little.

Chip scared her a little.

"So," he said, watching the grass fall, "we gonna be friends?"

"That," said Elly, "is for me to decide."

Fran started. She hadn't seen the others coming, and they were ranged now on the slope, Elly in front, the others fanned out raggedly behind her. Elly's dress, pink buds on white, slipped and swung in the breeze, making it seem as if she were moving when she wasn't moving at all. Maddy had a chocolate bar, Susan's hands were in fists, and Kitt was so mad there was a spot of white on each cheek. Fran didn't get it. Why were they so angry? What did she do now, break another one of their stupid rules? Why didn't they just leave her alone?

"Go away," she said.

"Shut up," Maddy answered around a bite of her candy. "I'll pound you."

"Chip," Elly said, "go away. We'll talk to Frances and see what we want."

Chip hugged his knees, looked at Fran, looked at the girls. He shook his head. "Nah, I don't think so."

Scowling, Elly took a step up. "You have to."

Fran grabbed Chip's arm. "My mother says I don't have to let anyone pick my friends for me if I don't want to."

Susan gasped, and Fran stared at her, puzzled, stared at Elly, whose hands clutched and twisted her skirt. She realized then that they weren't truly angry, just trying to be. What they really were was afraid. Scared to death. And that didn't make any sense at all.

"Go away," Elly said to Chip, her voice higher, softer, smaller. "Please go away."

Chip stood, and they backed off.

Fran pushed herself to her feet as a chill that wouldn't rub away walked her arms.

"Now look," Chip said, "I don't care what you think you did, or what you think you can do, Elly, but you did not pick Zera to be my friend. I did. Like I picked Susan's sister. You know that."

Elly shook her head.

Chip laughed. "You're a dope, you know it? A real dope." He looked at Fran. "So?"

Fran wanted to run; she wanted to stay; she wanted to laugh, and she wanted to stop the tears she saw filling Maddy's eyes. They were all acting like he was a ghost or something, and she had touched him, felt his arm, she knew he wasn't a ghost. He was as alive as they were.

As alive as Zera had been.

The sunlight died, summer died, and they were all in winter shadow in a slow winter wind that pushed at their hair and ruffled their clothes and blew dead leaves down the hill over browning grass. The sky was dark, but there were no stars. The only light left, the light that made them shadow, hid behind the trees and gave the trees sharp edges.

Fever dream.

"You made Zera die," she whispered.

Chip put his hands in his pockets, bent his head, looked at her sideways.

"You make Susan's sister die?"

Susan dropped to the ground, hugged her knees, rocked until Maddy dropped beside her and held her and let the tears slip out, one by one.

Winterlight.

"You're a ghost?"

Looking at him through gauze touched with red glitter, unable to run, unable to breathe except in shallow gulps. Unable to look away.

"I'm not a ghost," he said at last. "I am, that's all. I am." His gaze shifted to Elly when she stamped her foot in annoyance. "I'm a friend. A friend for life. Do *you* want to be my friend, Elly?"

The girl paled and stepped hastily backward until she bumped into Kitt, who shoved her away as if she had the plague.

Fever.

"Leave her alone," Fran snapped, and ran to Elly's side, put an arm around her waist. "Who'd want you for a friend? You're mean." She could feel her own tears surge, and subside. "Go away."

Chip straightened. "I'm there when you want me, and I go away when you don't. What's wrong with that?"

"Yeah, but when you go away for good," Fran said, "we get hurt and die, right?"

He didn't answer.

"That's dumb. That's a really dumb rule." Her arm slipped away from Elly's waist, but the girl grabbed her hand. "I think you should just go away and leave us alone."

The boy's face reddened. "But I don't have a friend!"

"Too bad." She shooed him. "Screw off, Chip, just screw off." She grinned at the others. "That's the way we do it in the city."

And when she looked back, he was gone.

Dream.

Winterlight fading; summerlight returning, and with it the heat and the bees and the sounds of the game down on the field. Fran felt her legs wobble a little, but Elly didn't release her, and the others quickly surrounded her, chattering, giggling nervously, searching the trees and the shrub until she suggested they go down to a kiosk and get a hot dog or something.

They ran.

Slipping, pushing, yelling all the way down the slope.

Running across the diamond and shrieking happily when the boys cursed and yelled at them.

Plowing through the bushes until they reached the blacktop path, darting around a woman with a baby carriage, kicking a soccer ball out of their way, nearly colliding with the refreshment stand when they reached it, then playfully shoving themselves into line, faces red, eyes shining.

Fran grinned, then laughed when Kitt said her mother was going to skin her alive when she got home tonight.

Elly tugged at her arm. "Do I have to wear a dress?"

"What? Don't be stupid. You don't have to wear a dress if you don't want to. That's silly."

Sodas. Hot dogs.

They stood to one side and didn't care about the mustard

dripping onto their chests, deciding that tomorrow, if they could get somebody to drive them, they'd go see the show out at the college.

"Boys!" Maddy cried.

They laughed and started for the exit.

"Thanks," Elly said when they reached Park Street, the others gone, waving good-bye.

Fran shrugged. "No problem." She checked the street in both directions. "See you tomorrow." And ran to the other side.

"Fran!"

She stopped and turned.

Elly stood on the curb. "I'm sorry," she called. "About all that stuff."

Fran nodded *it's okay* and backed away, ready to run, ready to fly home and tell her parents about the great time she'd had. Not about Chip, though. They'd think she was having another fever or something, lock her away until every doctor in the universe had had a look down her throat.

"Can I be your friend?"

Fran grinned, waved, and called a "Sure!" before she ran.

Ran a half dozen steps before turning around to wave again.

Elly was gone.

Nothing left but sharp edges, and the faint scent of cotton candy.

Lost in Amber Light

THERE WAS NO QUESTION THAT THE MUSIC DIDN'T FIT the night. It was too fast, too loud, too demanding. The band prancing on the portable stage at the back of the yard wore clothes that were too bright, too much like neon woven through itself, and even when they stood still there were spectral images of them hovering against the backdrop of heavily branched trees and thick shrubs nearly as high as small trees themselves. Speakers five feet tall shrieked. A single guitar note was a siren, an undulating bass too much a throbbing bomb, and the drummer wielded his sticks as if they were muskets crackling in the midst of ferocious battle. And all of it aided by strobe lights in blue and red, white and green, flailing the band and the dancers and the barely visible stars.

It was wrong.

All wrong.

On a night so warm and muggy, a languid breeze lazing through the upper branches, heat lightning now and then flaring on the horizon, crickets in the shadows, it should have been the blues. A saxophone, maybe a muted horn, talking music to the dark, keeping the dancing and the chattering and the movement slow. People would listen even when they weren't, feeling it inside where emotions weren't frantic but not always soothed, feeling melancholy or more tender without really knowing why.

It should have been the blues.

The night was too warm.

Less than an hour after the party had officially begun, Drake emptied a third glass of tepid red punch, threw a perfunctory smile at no one in particular, and wandered away, around the side of a house twice as large as any two on his block, reaching the front with a forced relieved sigh when the brick and wood and veined marble trim sliced the sound level in half, and half again. He didn't suppose anyone would miss him. There were more than fifty of them back there anyway, half strangers to one another, the rest too immersed in the music to give much of a damn. He stepped between two cars parked on the curving driveway and shoved his hands into his pockets. A glance over his shoulder, at the mansion, at the paving-stone path he had just taken, and he headed slowly for Williamston Pike, trying to figure out why he had bothered to come in the first place. Anita Atherton, after all, wasn't a close friend, or even a moderate acquaintance, and her cousin, Jill, who had asked him to come, was a royal, expert pain in the ass. Some of the time.

"Check it out," she had said last week. "You might meet someone you like."

He had doubted it then, doubted it more when he'd arrived and discovered that he was the only one in a suit, and knew it for sure when Anita, her birthday outfit more like a bikini with pretensions to a two-piece, shook his hand, kissed his cheek, and introduced him to her parents as someone else.

Halfway down the drive his tie was tucked into his jacket pocket, the jacket was slung over a shoulder, and he was working on an excuse to give his mother. Rain was out of the question; after the storms of last week there hadn't been a cloud in the sky, and she wasn't the kind to buy a miracle without reading the package first. A police drug raid was a little drastic. Food poisoning would freak her, she wouldn't go for a severe headache, and she definitely wouldn't believe that he had been bored.

It was hard, sometimes, having a mother who had more ambition than he did.

"Contacts, Drake," she had told him that morning. "It's important that a journalist have his contacts. Otherwise, where would he get his stories?"

"Mom."

An exasperated shrug followed by a patient sigh and a loving pat to his head. "Darling, it isn't as if you're a man of the world yet, you know. Something like this could give you the edge."

The worst part was, it almost made sense, and he hated it when she made sense. That meant he couldn't argue; and when he couldn't argue, he felt as though he were being manipulated. Controlled. He was damn near twenty and growing weary of being on a leash no matter how well-meaning, how liberal. He didn't always feel it, but he knew it was there.

The Pike was dark. Too many trees hid too many streetlamps, and the infrequent rumble of approaching automobiles always seemed to last just long enough to force him to turn around to see what it was. In the leaves blended into the black, night birds shifted, spoke in hushed bursts, sometimes exploded from the foliage and left falling twigs behind. Behind the hedge and stone walls of the estates lining the Pike, house lights flickered in the breeze that hadn't yet sifted down to his level, giving him the impression that there were men back there following him with lanterns and silent tracking dogs. Peasants after a monster. A posse tracking a killer. A procession of demonic monks looking for their equally demonic Master. It made him walk a little faster, made him wish there were sidewalks instead of just a dirt-and-pebble apron.

By the time he reached Park Street, he felt like a complete jerk for spooking himself.

A block later, he jumped when a tiny cry spun him around, looking for the hideous *thing*, whatever it was, that was after his blood, his life.

The streets were empty.

As far as he could tell, he was the only human left alive or moving in the world, and it wasn't even eleven o'clock. The dim glow of shoplights down Centre Street, the illuminated white face of the national bank's clock seemingly suspended in midair. A single globe of white over the post office entrance on the opposite corner. Everything else was black, in spite of the starlit sky.

The cry again, hollow in the silence that lay over the village, and he frowned, shifted his jacket off his shoulder, and peered at the library's lawn, looking for an animal of some kind, peered across the Pike looking for a lost child. Then he looked up, into the lower limbs of a spindly new maple growing by the curb, and grinned as much in relief as amusement.

"Well," he said, "you don't look so hot, pal."

Crouched in a wedge of three branches was a cat, larger than a kitten, much smaller than an adult. It cried again, softly, and tried to push into the trunk when he reached up. It hissed. It lashed a small white paw.

"Jungle cat," Drake said. "I thought you guys knew what you were doing."

The ears flattened; it hissed again.

He laughed quietly—mighty Simba waiting to pounce on unsuspecting prey. A step closer, and he saw the glint of a rhinestone stud on a leather collar. Mighty Simba got himself good and lost. And stuck.

He reached, and the paw lashed, just missing his thumb.

Leaving it here all night, he supposed, wouldn't be a crime; someone would probably help it in the morning. But there'd be traffic then, too, and he had a feeling that this cat wasn't yet wise to the ways of dodging speeding wheels.

"All right." He bunched the jacket in his hands. "Now, don't go having a cow or anything, pal, I'm only going to help you." He reckoned a short jump, a throw, a grab, and he'd have it down with no problem. "Just don't get all bent out of shape."

The cat watched him.

He jumped, threw, grabbed, and the cat wriggled immediately partway out of the jacket's folds. Drake stumbled backward when he landed, one hand instantly up to protect his face as the animal growled, lashed out, and raked needles across the side of his neck. He yelled and dropped the jacket. The cat landed with a sleeve draped over its head, shook it off, and dashed across the street, a single angry cry left behind. Drake swore at it as he snatched his jacket from the sidewalk, then gingerly tested his flesh for blood, vowing never to help animals again, they were never satisfied, they never even said thanks.

The cat yowled again, down the reach of an endless tunnel.

And quiet.

* * *

He glanced back the way he had come, stamped a heel for welcome noise, cleared his throat and walked on, past the post office, its white-framed windows paned not with glass but with still, black water that gave him no reflection when he looked, and that made him quickly check the pavement to make sure he still had a shadow. It was there. Only barely.

A shudder rolled his shoulders; he snapped his jacket like a whip and didn't like the sound.

Unlighted houses.

Maybe he should have stayed at the party, given it a second chance. Mingled a bit more, tried to fit in. But he hadn't even seen Jill, though she had promised to be there. Which, he realized, was typical. Though she had been in a few of his classes out at Hawksted, her attendance had always left something to be desired, forcing her to scramble every time a test was scheduled, a project due. What amazed him was that she passed. Every time. If he didn't work his head off, he'd be digging ditches for the state for a living, and wouldn't his mother just love that.

At Devon Street, he turned north and crossed the Pike, and stopped as soon as he had stepped over the curb.

Weak moonlight on the blacktop, on the concrete, but nothing else. Two houses up there should have been a light, an amber bulb over his front door. It was never out after dark. Never. His mother kept half a dozen spares on a shelf over the cellar stairs, and changed it regularly, once every six weeks whether it needed it or not. She switched it off only when she left for work in the morning or when she got up on weekends.

Now his house was as dark as the rest of the town, and he couldn't help feeling he'd made the wrong turn somewhere, right instead of left when he left Anita's house, or left instead of straight ahead after he'd rescued the young cat. This wasn't his street. It couldn't be. There was no light.

No light at all.

And when the feeling passed, he pinched his cheek, hard, to drive off the confusion. Not only was he spooking himself again, he was behaving like a jerk. He knew this was his block because, when he finally moved again, he could see the milk-can planters on Mrs. Loodeck's porch, the redwood glider on Mr. Tarman's porch across the street, and his own house with its turret on the left rear corner where his mother did her sewing, where his father had once tried to write the novel that would make them all wealthy. The three rosebushes in the front yard Mr. Bethune had planted for them two summers ago. The sagging second porch step. The unholy squeal of the screen door.

It was his block, his house.

Of course it was.

As he opened the inner door, he reached up and snapped a finger against the clear beveled glass that encased the amber bulb. Nothing happened. He snapped it again, harder, and the light flared on.

Sure it was.

And if he still doubted, which some timorous part of him did despite all evidence to the contrary, such doubts were thankfully erased when he paused in the front hall to let his vision adjust to the dark, heard a buzzing in the living room, looked in, and smiled. His mother was asleep on the couch, light blanket pulled to her chin, feet still in her slippers, the television on, sound low, picture nothing but rolling static. He switched it off, winked at the woman who had raised him alone since he was nine, and uttered a quick prayer of guilty gratitude that the inevitable inquisition would be postponed until morning. A can of soda snuck from the refrigerator. A stealthy climb up the staircase that expertly avoided all the ones that would creak betrayal. He undressed in the dark, went into the bathroom and closed the door, turned on the light.

"Oh swell," he muttered sourly when he saw the three red tracks on his neck. "A sloppy vampire."

What little blood there was had already dried to dark beads. He debated the use of medication for possible infection, decided against it, and went to bed, disdaining a sheet, burying his face in the pillow. A few minutes later, his mother came upstairs, and he sensed her out there, standing in his doorway, watching him, probably arguing with herself about waking him so she could find out what he had found out, then suggest a dozen ways how to do it better the next time he was asked.

Please, he thought.

She left him alone.

Shifting, then—first one leg, then the other, one arm, the other, flopping onto his back, arms out, palms up, the night breeze that had stalked him earlier working its way through the window screen and gliding over his stomach. A mosquito he killed with one rapid swipe.

Funny, sometimes, his mother was. Staying up as late as it took until he came home, then falling into bed, complaining about how tired she always was; never going out on dates, yet accepting an invitation to the Travelers just the other night, right out of the clear blue; questioning him about his own dates, and always forgetting their names; able to sell insurance with the best of them, yet never able to haggle with a shopkeeper or clerk.

The breeze tickled him.

Funny too about Jill; where the hell had she been?

But she could have been there. He'd spent most of his time standing around one of the long refreshment tables, noting faces, testing names against his memory, sipping, nibbling on sandwiches scarcely bigger than his palm, trying and unable to remember how Anita's father made his living. She could have been there and he simply hadn't seen her.

Did he care?

How much did he care?

He allowed his lungs a slow deep breath, a slower exhalation.

Not much, he admitted. She was fun to be around, but there was something about her, something tilted, that made him nervous. A sweet malice that he suspected was more than a little calculated.

His head rolled left so he could look out the window. A tree outlined by the moon, nothing more.

The breeze once more, a long strip of silk across his narrow chest that made him tremble.

He thought of the cat.

He remembered the lightless houses.

He turned away from the moon and stared at the wall until he fell asleep.

Something screamed in anguish.

Drake sat up, panting, wiped the sweat from his face with the corner of a sheet.

No sound.

He had been dreaming.

It couldn't have been the little cat.

Damp sheets in the morning, the floor sticky where it was bare. He could barely move, legs stiff from walking, bleary-eyed, head feeling as if he'd drunk wine instead of that godawful tepid punch. His jacket lay on the floor where he'd dropped it the night before, a long rip in the lining where the cat had thrashed its way clear. He rolled his eyes and hoped he could get it to the tailor's before his mother saw it. If not, there'd be a lecture on waste, carelessness, and the need to save money for the more important things in life. He loved his mother, but, lord, sometimes she acted more like a professor than someone who sold insurance.

The shower wasn't much better. No matter how hard he tried, he couldn't dry off. The day was too muggy, and morning hadn't even ended. He finally gave up and went downstairs in nothing but a pair of shorts, rehearsing what he'd tell her when the interrogation began. But she had already left for work, a scrawled note on the kitchen table telling him that she might not be home until late, her boss in the Harley office had decided it was time to catch up on the paperwork before they all smothered, be a dear and straighten up, Aunt Sheri and Uncle Wendall are coming to visit tonight, all the way from Pennsylvania, and she didn't want them to think she ran a slum here, be another dear and don't go far in case I don't get home in time to greet them.

Which meant, he thought glumly as he tossed the note away, his cousins would be here too. Private school brats on their way to the Ivy League and not afraid to let everyone know it. He would probably have to baby-sit for them, show them around, be their pal, introduce them to his friends, who would never let him forget it. Luckily, the Travelers was still around and he could kill at least one evening taking them over. After that, who the hell knew? Maybe he could mount an expedition into the cemetery at the end of the street. Preferably at midnight. Preferably ending with them falling into an open grave and breaking their necks.

"Right," he said to the empty house. "Sure."

On the other hand, who the hell was he kidding? He wouldn't do anything to them, and he wouldn't say anything no matter what the provocation. Visits like this were too important to his mother—a chance to prove to her family, for the millionth time, that she had indeed survived the desertion of her husband, and had done it well. Very well. She needed no one, wanted no one, and did not require the assistance of anyone, no matter how well-intentioned or how well meant.

Sometimes he hated those people for what they did to her.

He hated them more because he knew they blamed her. She had ambitions his father hadn't been able to handle. He wanted the kind of wife they used to have in the movies; she wanted a life outside the house. Even now, especially on days when everything went wrong and he wanted to bury himself in the cellar until his luck changed, he could hear echoes of the arguments, the fights, that had kept him awake at night, that erupted during meals, that finally became one long campaign of marital warfare.

She wouldn't leave; he wouldn't leave.

Drake spent a lot of time with his friends, eating there, sleeping over, avoiding the Devon Street house until, at last, something broke. He never knew what happened, but one night he came home, and his father was gone.

He had wept.

So had his mother, and two days later got her first job.

He cleaned, then, and mowed the lawn, took another shower and swept the porch. When he was finished, he checked the refrigerator for something to drink, closed the door, opened it again and groaned. His mother had forgotten to do the shopping the day before; there was nothing for supper.

"You're fired, Mom," he muttered, and since she would be late, he knew she wouldn't have time to pick something up on the way home. Which meant that he would have to turn himself into Drake Saxton, Fearless Shopper, and go down to Bueller's Market. She hated it when he did, he knew it, and loved it. More often than not, he blew the weekly meal budget out of the water in one gluttonous trip, lugging home his favorite foods, healthy or not, and a dozen things that had looked good at the time but would seldom be eaten by either one of them.

It drove her crazy.

The last time she complained, he said, "Mom, I'm just a kid, what do I know about nutrition? Maybe you should get a husband."

She threw a loaf of bread at him.

He ran out of the house ahead of her laughing curses, came home an hour later with a gallon of her favorite ice cream.

A T-shirt fished out of a dresser drawer, tennis shoes without socks, and he walked down to the market, thinking he ought to get nothing but peanut butter and jelly, it would serve them right. Unfortunately, it had better be steaks, potatoes in the microwave quick and easy, with a big salad to keep things cool.

Heavens, Aunt Sheri would say, *what a sumptuous meal. You must be doing well, dear, selling all that insurance. How wonderful for you. Has Wendall told you about that office building he designed for those Mormon people in Memphis? You wouldn't believe all the trouble they gave him. Tell her all about it, Wendall.*

Uncle Wendall would eat and say nothing; it would all be in his eyes.

Barbi would say, *Aunt Rene, it looks terrific, but I'm still on that silly diet, can I just have the salad, would you mind?*

Yeah, Deena would echo, *can I just have the salad? Mother, the Mormons are not terrible people. They're just fussy, that's all.*

And Chuck would mimic his father, eating the meat and not caring if it had been cooked.

I wonder, Drake thought, if there's a train out of here this afternoon. Preferably to Cheyenne.

The market wasn't much better when he got there. It wasn't a large place, and the already narrow aisles were crowded with haphazard displays as well as shoppers, most of whom seemed to have come in just to take advantage of the air-conditioning. By the time he reached the meat counter, his ribs had taken a beating, the food basket he held was damn near breaking his arm, and the smells of everything from freshly ground coffee to the ammonia cleaner used on the floor had begun to give him a headache. It didn't help to see a roast pig's head staring at him from a bed of crushed ice and parsley.

"You ever eat one of them things?" a rasping voice said beside him.

The butcher, apron begrimed and straw hair straggling damply from under a crushed white cap, took his order with a flat grunt, and a swipe of a thick, tattooed forearm over his mouth.

"Not on a bet," Drake answered. He turned his head and grinned at Kayman Kalb.

Kalb grinned back from under a backward-turned baseball cap. "Looks like my first wife." His plaid shirt was open, abundant chest hairs white, the chest itself still muscular though

Drake knew the man had to be at least sixty-five. "Never could keep her mouth shut. You ever gonna get married?"

"I have to graduate first."

"Oh. Right." A thick finger poked his arm. "You ever want to write a feature story about me, just give me a holler. Financial wizard makes a fortune making chairs. Hell of a story. Give me a call, boy. Always glad to help the press."

Drake nodded, grabbed his package from the counter when the butcher slapped it down—another grunt, another swipe—and made his way to the register, set by the entrance. The clerk took her time, chatting gaily, exclaiming over a squealing baby in a backpack, commiserating over food prices, finally asking Drake if he was expecting company or just stuffing himself tonight.

"Relatives, Roxy," he said to the buxom redhead, who more than once figured in his summer dreams.

"Too bad."

"You're telling me."

"Have them for stew," Kalb called from somewhere down the line. "Lots of salt. They always need lots of salt."

Laughter clung to him as he stepped back outside and sighed at the weight the sun dropped on his shoulders. The glare off the sidewalk made him squint, and he stayed close to the curb, trying to keep in the shade, where it wasn't all that much cooler.

Alaska, he thought; tomorrow, I'm getting Mom to take us right to Alaska to live in an igloo and the hell with Wendall Firth and all his little Firths even if Aunt Sheri was his mother's sister.

A cat whimpered behind a hedge.

He wasted ten minutes trying to find it.

By the time he reached home, blood from the fresh meat began seeping through the bottom of the brown paper bag.

At six o'clock the telephone rang.

"You've got to be kidding," he said, giving the living room window his best martyr's expression.

"There's nothing I can do about it, dear, I'm sorry."

"But Mom, that means they may not be here until midnight."

His irritation pricked the back of his neck when she reminded him, too calmly for him to miss her own agitation, that Wendall's car breaking down wasn't her fault, don't pout over things you can't do anything about.

Which was, he thought after he replaced the receiver, the whole problem with the world. He stomped into the kitchen and sneered at it. Control. Give him a little control, just once, and things would soon change around here, by Christ. Drake Saxton, Temporary King of the Whole Goddamn World.

Damn.

He watched the early news, the national and world news, stood up from the couch every time he heard a car turn into the street; he stood on the porch and watched Mrs. Loodeck water her plants, billowing floral bathrobe wrapped around a body almost as wide as her front door; Mr. Tarman oiled his glider, the way he did every week, then wiped it down with a chamois; the sun dropped behind the houses across the street, blanking their faces; a pair of terriers trotted up toward the graveyard, tails high, tongues hanging brightly; the sky bled away its light slowly and the breeze finally died.

The television gave him game shows he couldn't bring himself to watch.

His mother called again, apologizing, she wouldn't be home for at least two or three more hours.

"You getting overtime?"

She laughed. "Grey hair, dear, just more grey hair."

He called Jill, for no other reason than he was tired of pacing, tired of sitting, tired of trying to find things to do. There was no control; it was driving him nuts.

"So," he said after running the gauntlet of her ever-suspicious father, "you busy tonight?"

"Of course I am," she said. "It's summer, you idiot. I've got stuff going every night and twice on Saturdays."

"You want to go to the Travelers?"

"Sure, what time?"

He checked his watch and closed one eye. "Eight-thirty, half an hour. I can't stay very late, though."

"How come?"

"Company coming."

"So why are you leaving?"

He didn't know; he stayed silent.

"No problem. Where?"

"Meet you at the gate?" He'd been to her house once, and that had been enough. Mr. Nowell had been worse than Aunt Sheri, quizzing him on everything except his weight and birthstone.

She giggled. "Okay. Dutch?"

He feigned indignance. "I am perfectly capable of arranging entrance payment for both of us, Miss Nowell, thank you very much."

"Wow, is that reporter talk?"

"Later," he said, and hung up, looked down at his feet and slapped his forehead. "So what the hell made you do a dumb-ass stupid thing like that, Saxton? You're asking for trouble, you know. Jesus, you're a jerk."

He went upstairs to change, checkered shirt and jeans, and to arrange the mess of undistinguished brown hair he'd obviously gotten from his father.

"Suppose," he said to the bathroom mirror, "Mom gets home before you do? She will, you know. You'll be in deep shit."

His hair refused to obey, and he finally let it flop over his ears, over his brow, as usual. Next year he was getting a crew cut and the hell with Oxrun fashion.

"Suppose," he said to the sink as he leaned over the counter, writing a note to explain where he was, when he'd be home, but not why he had gone, "Uncle Wendall gets here first and you're not here? Then what? Mom comes home, they're all sitting around the porch with their bags on the lawn, she'll hunt you down and murder you."

He almost changed his mind.

It wouldn't be fair to let her face them alone.

Darling, Aunt Sheri would say, that goddamn finger pressed against her cheek the way it always did when she looked at something that disturbed her by its very existence, *it's such a shame you have to work so late just to make ends meet. Isn't it, Wendall. Isn't it a shame? I don't mean to pry, dear, but maybe it's time Drake took a job instead of all those extra classes. Don't you think so, Chuck? Don't you think Drake could sacrifice just a little bit to help his mother out?*

Of course, they hadn't been around when his father didn't come home. They called once a month, they scattered blame like it was corn seed, but aside from a fifty-dollar check that first Christmas, no one had given them a hand but themselves.

He made sure he had his house key and wallet, turned on the outside light, and locked the door behind him.

The street was already dark.

Again, all the lights were out.

He looked up at the amber bulb, scowled, flicked the globe with his thumb twice before it came on, and took a deep breath.

Go?

You're already there, he answered, and left.

She was two inches taller, even in her flats, her white shirt more snug than his, her white shorts cut high and loose, her hair against her tan a deep golden brown. A round face, a pug nose, a thin scar that ran from the corner of her right eye almost to her ear, making that eye seem almost slanted. She played basketball, swam, hiked in the White Mountains, and was reputed to have beaten up every boy on her block every year until she reached high school.

When she took his hand, her grip was gentle.

They didn't say anything beyond grins for *hi*. Drake was somewhat astonished that she'd shown up at all, and didn't want to press his luck scaring her off with some brilliantly stupid remark.

It didn't matter.

For most of the first half hour she did all the talking for them, telling him about the supreme bust her cousin's party was, how she'd left after five minutes to go to a movie that wasn't so hot either, that she was, really, no shit, sorry she'd made him go and then left without even seeing him.

While he told her about Uncle Wendall and the rest of the Firths, she dragged him to a bunting-draped stand to show him how to shoot spinning targets, marching ducks, twirling bears, and a scarecrow that had five crows perched on each straw arm. He cheered her on, carried the panda she won, and let her rush him down a lane to a baseball toss, dropping nine in a row into a canted, narrow-mouthed garbage can. He carried the giant canary and followed her to a snack concession where she treated him to spicy hot dogs and diet soda, never once slowing down long enough for him to tell her about the family about to invade the Saxton fortress.

She kissed his cheek and said she thought no offense but his relatives sounded like class-A assholes.

She dunked a clown in a water tank by using a pool ball to hit a bull's-eye no larger than his palm.

She kissed his cheek when he gave the panda to a little girl who couldn't seem to stop crying.

They reached the oval close to ten, and he balked when she headed straight for the Octopus.

"No."

"Why not, Drake?" She leaned close; he smelled heat and sugar.

"I don't like that thing, that's all."

"Oh, come on, it won't kill you."

Doubtfully, he watched the round-bottom cars swing and spin up into the shadows above the carnival light, saw the faces desperate to have fun, heard the obligatory shrieks. He shook his head again.

"Drake," she said, sternly as she smiled, "it's okay, really. Millions of people ride it every night." Close again. "You can sit in my lap." Her arm draped across his shoulders. She licked her lips and whispered, "I'll let you feel me up a little." Waggled her eyebrows. Kissed his cheek.

And will you wipe my mouth when I dribble ice cream, Mommy? he thought, suddenly annoyed.

"The carousel," he said, pulling her toward the back.

"Oh, Jesus, wimp city."

"My choice for a change," he said as lightly as he could. "Give the wimp a break, okay?"

He could see it, then—hurt, is he joking, hurt, a shade of anger, finally deciding Drake doesn't hurt people so why the hell not.

"And who," she wanted to know as they joined the short line, "ever heard of a black merry-go-round? It's almost obscene, don't you think?"

He loved it.

So black, so deeply and unrelentingly black, the strings of lights ranged along its circus-top roof seemed to float above it, the fall of light beneath the canopy soft enough to touch. The animals perfectly carved, gaily painted, even the bench seats in emerald and gold seemed alive somehow.

"I'll bet there isn't even a brass ring or anything," she complained when they finally reached the platform and the carousel slowed, the music slowed.

"Sue me," he told her, poking her sharply with a thumb.

"Damn right."

On then, struggling through the red-faced kids streaming off, walking counterclockwise around the base until she found a mustang with a purple mane for her, and a rearing stag with ruby horns for him. Her expression dared him to fault her; he kissed her cheek mockingly and climbed aboard.

"You know," she said as the mustang began to rise, the music began to play, "you could write about this for the paper."

"Why? It's just a carnival."

She shook her head, held on to the brass pole with one hand and leaned precariously over. "I mean, you could do the history of these things, y'know? What they mean to outlying places like the Station, stuff like that."

Pieces of him swept by on his left, the mirrors taking him, absorbing him, bringing him back for more.

"Boring."

"Hey," she said, straightening so abruptly he thought at first she was angry, "if you're going to be a reporter, Saxton, you've got to get yourself a little imagination, right? I mean, you going to write about proms and professors and pay hikes all your life?"

He couldn't answer.

She obviously didn't expect one.

His hands on the pole, sliding up, sliding down, while he thought about wishing wells and magic lamps and the music that sounded like tin and silver, pans and bells, while the wind pushed the hair from his eyes and rippled his shirt and opened his mouth so he could gulp it in like water, while he rode the stag and wanted to ride it all night, away from the carousel, away from the Station and into the hills where the trees would hide him and the hunters couldn't find him and the weather would be the only thing that would tell him where to go;

while he watched the other riders always ahead, always behind, never looking back, always looking in the mirrors, while those on the ground moved away from his speed, from his antlers, from his hooves, not quite cheering, not quite screaming, not quite afraid and too afraid to run, while the music, tin and silver, rendered him deaf to everything but the cry of a young cat trapped in the branches of a young tree in a town too old to be anything but just there;

while the music slowed and the stag slowed and his eyes watered until his forearms, first one, then the other, wiped them clear.

"Jesus," he whispered, and climbed down, stood for a moment until his legs stopped trembling. "God."

Jill didn't seem to notice. "Octopus," she demanded, payment for, and he watched her climb into the saucer-shaped car, watched the car lift, watched her blow him a kiss before the speed kicked in and she had to hang on. Nothing to see, then, and nothing to hear but the screams until it slowed, gears and chains grinding, and she pantomimed a message: *I'm going around again.* He felt like a jerk. People were probably watching him watching her, nudging each other and smirking. He's down here, she's up there, we all know who wears the pants in that family.

He walked away, paused at several food stands without buying a snack, exchanged smiles with a few people he knew, although vaguely, and finally left the oval, back onto the midway where he kept to one side and read the signs, listened to the spiels, realized he'd left the canary somewhere behind, surrendered to a sudden urge like the jerk of a string and entered a square tent that smelled of sawdust and fresh paint.

It was empty.

It was dark.

But not so dark that he couldn't see a woman standing in the distance, a silhouette against lighter black. Watching him. He knew she was watching him.

Cautiously, not sure how dangerous moving around in here was, he walked toward her, frowning, head slightly forward in an effort to see better, wondering if she was part of the show or only another customer wondering the same as he.

She didn't move.

His left hand reached out timidly, searching for something to touch, grip, brush against, and found nothing.

She didn't move.

A few moments later he collided with something hard that whacked across his thighs, made him grunt, made him snatch at it and realize it was a small folding chair with a thin padded seat. Hanging on to the back, he glanced around, saw nothing, no one else, and shrugged as he sat, intending to remain for only a few seconds, until his senses were able to give him bearings, better vision.

She didn't move.

"Hello?" he said.

The light behind her, neither from above nor below, brightened enough for him to see that she wore a ballgown, strapless shoulders, hooped skirt with tiers of stiff ruffles, a broad red ribbon that tied her hair behind her ears. Hands clasped demurely at her waist. Powdered bosom pushed in, pushed up, barely contained and not at all exciting.

"Hello?"

Her face in shadow.

He knew her.

Leaning forward again didn't help him to see, but he knew her and couldn't bring her name, conjure her features. It was the stance, for some reason. Not in those clothes, but it was the stance that nearly gave her away.

"Hey, what . . . am I supposed to do something?"

No echo, no indication of space, no volume.

He might have been sitting alone in a closet, or in a monstrous empty stadium.

She turned sideways.

In profile, a long nose with a faint bump and the bridge and a delicate hook on the end, a chin that pointed out, lips in an unconscious disapproving purse. Lower, to a bulging stomach the gown couldn't restrain.

"My god," he whispered.

It was Sheri Firth.

Keeping a hand on the chair's back, he stood and glanced around, trying to decipher the joke here, searching for the others. "Aunt Sheri?" The dark was too intense; he sat again, heavily, wiped his hands on his legs. "Aunt Sheri, what's going on? What the hell are you doing here? Mom—"

"Don't swear," she said quietly, clearly. "Wendall, please tell the little snot not to swear at me."

"Why the hell aren't you at the house?" he demanded, wanting to stand and not wanting to give her the satisfaction. "Mom's going to be worried. She already is." There was no sense looking for her husband; it was too dark. "Where's Uncle Wendall?"

"Speak when you're spoken to, you little bastard."

Turning her back to him.

Bitch, he thought.

"I heard that, Drake," she said.

"Okay," he said. "Bitch." And he winced.

Turning again. Right profile.

"It isn't my place to criticize, of course," she said, her lips barely moving, "but it seems to me you ought to be home now, taking care of your mother."

"She's working. For Christ's sake, what are you doing here? Is this some kind of joke?"

Facing him.

Face in shadow.

"The meat you bought at that little pathetic place you call a market is tough. I'll never be able to eat it, you know that. Give it to me raw and it'll still taste like old leather. I simply won't have it."

"What—"

"And most of that lettuce has brown edges. Two days old, at least. Wendall doesn't like brown edges. And he certainly won't eat that ridiculous steak. You'll have to think of something else."

He did stand then, lashed a foot out to kick the chair away.

It was gone.

He heard music: a tune he didn't recognize, but it was as if someone had dragged the carousel's band of bears in here with them. When he looked back, his aunt was dancing, waltzing with an invisible partner, the partner not very close. It was all very formal; it was all very disturbing.

"Aunt Sheri, this is stupid."

The dark was warm, chilled, felt like air and felt like wool.

She danced a little faster, skirts rustling, feet scraping across a rough dirt floor.

His hands clenched and opened, his head swiveled left and right, but he couldn't leave. A step backward, a second, a third, suggested he could get away, get outside, any time he wanted to, but as he watched his aunt whirl with a ghost in large circles against the dim light, he simply couldn't leave.

Couldn't look away.

The music, tin and silver.

"Aunt Sheri?"

Couldn't see her face.

This was nuts. She was going to kill herself if she didn't stop, she was going to get hurt. He didn't know who had thought up this insane gag, but he'd had enough. He strode several paces to the left, swatting at the air, heedless of what might happen should he strike a support post, a wall, someone else standing in here watching the macabre show; a dozen paces more, looking up, looking out, seeing neither ceiling nor walls and not feeling anything but a pleasant chill. Like a breeze.

Realizing that the light always stayed behind his aunt.

Dancing faster.

Face in shadow.

Trotting in hopes of getting behind her—this was ridiculous; jogging easily—this was nuts; suddenly sprinting as though he would catch the trick and trickster unaware. Spiraling inward in order to grab hold of his aunt. Nothing changed. When he slowed, she spun, in perfect time to the music almost fast enough now to lose all semblance of a tune.

Tin and silver.

Panting at last, he sagged to his knees, a hand pressed against his side, face toward the ceiling as his mouth worked for a breath.

"Hey!" he yelled. "Hey, get in here!"

No one answered; no one came.

A skittering across the dirt, and something bumped against his leg. A shoe. Her shoe. Sensible, as always, and as always, expensive.

This is a dream, he thought, and felt stupid for thinking it. They were always dreams, the nightmares and wishes and scenes that weren't real; they were always dreams, and the dreamer always woke up and sometimes was glad and sometimes was sorry. But the point was—they were dreams.

He saw the other shoe fly off into the light, fading, shrinking, never hitting the back wall. Vanishing.

"Aunt Sheri?" His voice small. Helpless. "Please, Aunt Sheri?"

She tried to speak; the words were garbled; the music played faster.

Why doesn't she fall?

She danced on, back perfectly straight, arms in perfect position to hold on to her partner.

He cried for help.

The light turned amber, his shadow-aunt darkened.

He called out a second time, and the first drop of blood landed on his cheek.

He reared back, twisted away, and the first shard of her gown fluttered into the air, absurdly slowly, absurdly long.

Ignoring the taste of bile in his mouth, the surge of acid in his stomach, he scrambled to his feet and tried to reach her, changed his mind and tried to run away, but the blood was faster and the gown fell apart and his aunt danced on to the music tin and silver; he screamed at her to stop and received gibberish in turn.

Face in shadow.

Dancing on.

He found the chair and grabbed it, knelt beside it, pulled himself onto it and covered his face with his hands.

He heard her bare feet on the dirt, heard the blood splatter, heard the silk and satin tatter, heard the music.

Heard the first of her bloodless skin pull away from her arm.

He moaned.

He rocked.

Mom, he prayed; Mom, Jesus Christ, what's going on?

The music stopped.

The sound of a distant wind, not approaching, simply traveling, winding down to the hiss of a breeze in summer leaves, winding down to silence.

His fingers spread, stiffly as if cramped.

His shirt, his jeans, were drenched; he could feel the blood drying in his hair. An image of himself in gleaming red made him retch, but nothing came up, and he swallowed as rapidly as he could as tears finally broke and crawled down his cheeks.

One eye opened—a lost little child in a theater, not wanting to see the monster, too curious to look away—and saw a stick figure frozen in the midst of an extravagant sweep of its arms, accepting plaudits from admirers for the magnificence of its dance.

A giggle was swallowed. Another escaped, and that horrified him more than what was left of his aunt, standing there, frozen, in the middle of the light.

Dreamer.

A slow inhalation brought him out of the chair, another one with a hand pressed against his chest moved him a step forward, turning slightly sideways as if ready to run away, blinking, reaching out.

Touching the light.

It was solid.

He pressed harder; it was cool.

He ran his fingers along its unblemished surface as he circled the indistinct figure inside. But it was his aunt. He knew it. There was too much arrogance in that stance, too much preparation.

The light went out.

He nearly fell as he whirled, and saw an exit sign right behind him.

Tell someone, he thought, hysteria and panic close to hand; tell someone what happened, Jesus, tell Mom.

He ran outside, and grabbed a guy wire with both hands to stop himself, swinging himself around until the wire started to burn.

The midway was deserted.

Bewildered, he checked his watch, and didn't believe the Travelers had closed just before eleven. Then he brought the hand close to his eyes, turned his arm over, stretched it out, brought it back. He sagged against the taut wire. There was no blood. He checked his shirt, jeans, hair, spun around with a question opening his mouth and saw that the tent flap had been sewn closed with tarnished copper cable.

He had to tell his mother what had just happened. Or Jill. Yes; Jill was closer. She was on the Octopus, he'd only been gone fifteen minutes, no more, though it seemed like hours, and there was no way she would be content with only one ride. She knew about weird things; she'd be able to help him out, think of an explanation of either what had just happened, or how he'd been taken.

The police; he'd have to tell them, too. His aunt was dead, entombed in that tent.

He looked at it.

The wind kicked up, and sun-faded pennants along the rim snapped at him, the sides of the canvas billowed toward him.

He stumbled more than ran, thumbs brushing the tears away harshly.

"Here," a voice whispered.

He waved a hand—*not now*.

"Here," it insisted.

He hurried on toward the oval; the voice followed.

"God damn," he said, nearly shouting, turned to the speaker, and Jill handed him an ice-cream cone.

"Strawberry," she said. "You like it?"

He nodded, examined it, sniffed it, tasted it, nodded again. "Real strawberries in here. That's the best kind."

"A connoisseur, huh?"

"Years of practice."

She couldn't quite look at him. "Are you all right?"

A wan smile quickly vanished. A shrug.

"You're mad," she said, a finger tracing the length of her scar. "I'm sorry. Really. I just couldn't resist that thing. I don't blame you for leaving, are you sure you're all right?"

He watched without seeing the people pushing by, checked the sky, realized they were standing in front of an undecorated caravan with a sign that declared that this was where lost things and people were found and held.

Another shrug. How, honestly, could he be mad when he had known what he was getting into when he asked her out? She was Jill, that's all there was to it, and if he hadn't wanted to abide her he could have come alone.

"You're dripping."

Ice cream trailed down the cone and over the back of his hand coldly. He licked it quickly and, at the same time, let his expression tell her he was okay, don't worry, and he wasn't mad at all.

Relieved, she took his arm, and they bucked the surging customer river to a clear space on the other side, where he pointed out a grey-board shack that claimed to hold a photography studio where, when they entered, they discovered cardboard people in bathing suits, garish military uniforms, space suits, elaborate antebellum gowns and evening dresses, or nothing at all, with holes where their faces should have been. Jill pointed at one nude woman with hands on her hips, the hips thrust forward, and allowed that, all modesty aside, her own figure was rather better than that. Drake fought the urge to compare openly, fought back a maddening blush when he lost and did it anyway, then hastily, solemnly, concentrated on a grizzled backwoodsman with an eyepatch and noted that the man's coonskin cap seemed to be a little ragged.

Jill playfully bumped him with a hip, laughing quietly, knowing.

On the walls, framed black-and-white pictures to prove how the real and the false were all the same to the camera when the colors were gone.

Jill walked a circle around the nude. "I think I'll do it," she decided, idly scratching a hip. "It'll drive my father up the wall."

"I'll wait outside." He backed into a muscleman and had to grab it before it fell. He pointed to the exit. She put her face in the hole and stretched her arms around the cardboard until her hands modestly covered the painted breasts.

"Better?"

She winked.

Oh my god, he thought, and once outside heard a hoarse voice whisper, "Hey, over here."

He scowled.

His eyes widened.

The midway was empty, the photography shop locked, the concessions boarded up.

"Here."

A gust turned him, prodded him forward, until he collided gently with an empty platform he hadn't noticed before. Behind it, another tent, smaller than the first, its front painted to depict a Wild West show. Cowboys, Indians, the cavalry charging, while off to the side were snowcapped mountains, a young woman in settler's dress, a squaw washing clothes in a shallow stream. Buffalo Bill. Annie Oakley.

"Here."

No one there.

The flap was open.

He called Jill.

A whisper: "Here."

The sound of a small cat yowling inside.

The bleachers took up all of one side, eight rows high, the wood unpainted and worn smooth, creaking softly when he stepped into the first row and sat down. He didn't know why he did. He had no business in here, waiting for some stupid cowboy show when he should be outside, hunting for Jill, a cop, anyone at all. In fact, he shouldn't even be on the carnival grounds. If he had any brains, he would get the hell away, run like hell to the police station, and bring someone back. Sitting here was dumb. But he didn't move because that voice had been speaking to more parts of him than he had realized existed, parts of him that had already begun to hint that he didn't need anyone's goddamn help, that he knew damn well what was going on and all he had to do was think about it for a while and it would come to him, like an epiphany that would rip the dark from his vision and let him see, for the first time, what he had only suspected was there.

And the minute he thought it, his spine became rigid, his mouth opened just a little as he struggled to understand.

That scared him.

When he didn't even make sense to himself, there was something far more wrong here than watching his aunt disintegrate in a nightmare. And he wouldn't figure it out this way, panting slightly, pushing his tongue into his cheek, letting his hands knead his thighs.

He had to be calm.

He had to find distance.

He had to be objective is what it was, practice what he'd learned in class, in his occasional work for the *Station Herald,* in the lectures he had heard from visiting reporters from cities that had blocks with more people than the Station. He had to be composed. He had to ignore the slow growing light that illuminated what seemed to be a circus ring filled with desert sand, a cactus here and there, and far at the back a vulture sitting on the only branch left on a long-dead tree. He had to close his mind to what was obviously some sort of hallucination, maybe brought on by the dizzying carousel ride, and retrace his way through the fear and find only the facts. He couldn't watch the two cowboys strolling toward each other from either side of the ring. He couldn't permit himself to recognize the paunchy, slope-shouldered, gait of his uncle, or the insolent stride of cousin Chuck, flab noticeable even with the loose clothing he wore, though he had to admit that the characteristic stubble of beard on the kid's acne-scarred face fit this scene better than it did when he wore his usual white sweater and white slacks.

Facts.

He had to understand the facts, shred the fancy, dispel the childhood notion that these two men, in near perfect silence, were about to have an old-fashioned, Hollywood shoot-out. Right here. Right in front of him. The vulture's wings flapping in anticipation. Dust rising from their dusty boots. His uncle spitting to one side. His cousin spitting toward his father. The hollow stamp of their boots on the sandy soil, the leather creak of their gunbelts. Stopping. Glowering at each other. Chuck adjusting his hat as if shading his eyes from a sun Drake couldn't see. Wendall leaning over without taking his gaze from the kid to adjust the rawhide strap holding his holster against his thigh.

Drake jumped to his feet and said, "Hey—"

They drew and fired.

No echo, no sensation of sound in a large cave.

The pistols fired.

Nothing more.

Wendall's head snapped back as his left eye was shot out.

Chuck doubled over, his free hand grabbing at the hole in his belly.

Drake screamed as they fell, as the light shifted to amber, and he tripped over an iron brace, sprawled and yelled when his elbow caught the edge of the seat. He cupped it with his other hand, pushed up to his knees and didn't look at the circus ring.

The vulture cried softly. Its wings flapped like canvas.

Drake crawled on knees and one hand to the exit and fell outside where the wind slapped him with dust, and a voice whispered, "Here."

The oval was quiet, all the rides empty and in their places, waiting for new riders; a fruit-punch machine at a food stand bubbling untended, the smell of frying hamburgers, popcorn bouncing softly against the plastic sides of its cooker.

Okay, he thought, shivering against the wind, his face gleaming with perspiration; all right, no problem, she's already gone, I'll just go home too.

He listened for sounds of voices, footsteps, hoping for a moment that there was a special show in the arena, so special that even the carnival's workers were there. He listened as he backed out of the oval, and knew he was kidding himself. He was alone. Whatever had happened wasn't any stupid god-damn special show, and it wasn't a nuclear holocaust, and it wasn't a dream, because his throat was raw from the screaming he had done and the screaming he held back, his elbow still ached, his stomach was filled with acid that made him spit several times, and if it wasn't a dream, then what the hell was it?

A monochrome picture of a nude woman suddenly danced in front of him. Unwillingly he took it, held it at arm's length, brought it close to his eyes, turned to Jill and said, "You're putting on weight."

She slapped his shoulder.

He laughed and stuffed the picture into his hip pocket.

"Going to put it under your pillow?"

"I'm going to show it to my uncle and tell him you're my girlfriend and you do this for a living."

She didn't say anything.

Damn, he thought the moment he saw her eyes; your foot, you jackass, is now firmly between your teeth.

And an instant later: holy shit, she's not kidding. Oh Jesus, Saxton, what have you gotten yourself into now?

They turned into a narrow lane, not as crowded though no less noisy.

"I've been thinking about your company," she said, neatly sliding away from a child racing a balloon.

"So have I," he answered morosely. "I'm going to have to go soon, or I'm dead meat."

"No offense, Drake, but maybe that's what they need."

"What?" He stopped and was nearly run over by a baby carriage. A muttered apology to the mother, a quick trot to catch up to Jill. "What are you talking about?"

"You're too nice to them."

"Like hell."

Her head tilted toward him. "So who bought the steaks, the

veggies, the salad stuff, huh? God, if they come that late, a sandwich will do, for god's sake. They'll be exhausted anyway, they won't feel like eating."

"My mother—"

"Didn't tell you to buy a ten-course meal."

"Well . . ."

She sidestepped in front of him, put her hands on his shoulders and wouldn't let him pass. "Drake, come back to the world for a minute, okay? You're a great guy, no shit, but sometimes you can be so goddamn dense." A knuckle rapped his forehead. "I'll bet your teen-year rebellion was refusing to pick up your socks."

Annoyed at her intrusion, oddly pleased that she seemed to care enough to make it, he snatched her wrist. Hesitated. Then tugged gently, and her face came down and he kissed her lips, far longer than he had intended.

When he pulled away, she blinked as if swimming out of a minor daze.

"Jesus, Drake," she whispered.

The carnival sighed around them.

"Yeah," he whispered back.

In the background, the carousel.

"All right, come on," she said at last, grabbing his hand and elbow, "I want you to see this incredible game place I found last week. It's sort of like bobbing for apples, except they're greased tennis balls or something. You can win ten bucks if you get three in five minutes without drowning."

He shook his head; it was getting late.

She yanked; he followed, and couldn't help watching the way her buttocks stretched her shorts in such a tantalizing way that he began to wonder if he'd secretly been raised as a monk. Was this the first time he'd really seen what she looked like?

When a crowd of teenagers swarmed around them, the grip was broken and Jill was carried away, one arm up, commanding him to follow.

And for just that second, the hand, the arm, the manner, reminded him of his mother.

Come along, Drake, dear, we don't have much time.

The hell with you, he thought; damnit, the hell with you.

His own about-face startled him so much that he was afraid to look over his shoulder. Instead, he returned to the midway, seething over the playful scolding, confused over the kiss, wishing he'd never come in the first place, it would have been a lot easier just to stay at the house and stay bored until someone, anyone, came home.

But she was right in one respect—being nice sometimes made him look like a jerk, transformed him into a doormat. Until now that had been a small price to pay. Until now he hadn't seriously considered taking control.

Idiot; you're an idiot and they're all laughing.

He skipped once as if ready to run, skipped again and did run through the crowd until the crowd slipped away and left him alone with the wind and the sound of his ragged breathing.

Down the center of the midway, then, dodging a paper cup blown across his path, hurdling a toppled stroller, its tiny wheels spinning. He looked neither left nor right. He ignored the gunshot snaps of flags and loose canvas. He refused to look at the sky, at the colored lights. A scrap of paper crawled after him, clung to his ankle and slipped away. He didn't look at it. He kept his head up, his attention on the gate at the midway's far end, at the suggestion of trees beyond it, because the trees meant that behind them were the houses, the streets, the people who had somehow disappeared from the field.

A voice called his name.

He didn't look.

A woman called his name.

He didn't look.

Nor did he allow himself to think about anything but running without falling. Not headlong, just steady. Shaking his head once to flip the sweat from his eyes. Not sprinting, just escaping. Holding his right arm tight against his side for several yards to stifle a painful stitch that threatened to slow him down.

A woman called his name.

Go away, he yelled at her, and not making a sound; get away, I don't know you!

But he saw her.

Twenty yards ahead, on his left, on a long narrow stage in front of a flat-topped tent badly painted to resemble an oasis, its pool of water peeling, camels more like horses, childlike suggestions of robed Arabs reclining under palm trees much too stiff and dark. In front of her was a straw basket fat and low, its top tilted to one side, something dark moving just below the lip.

For some reason it didn't surprise him that the woman was Deena, the attractive one, the cousin he had the most fun with because she never seemed to take her parents seriously, the one who had never blamed him for his father's leaving. She wore pale-blue harem pants and a matching skimpy top, a white veil over her nose and mouth and somehow pinned in her hair. Arms lined with gold bracelets. Feet bare. Swaying, hands writhing, fingers beckoning, eyes lined to increase their size and staring at him as he approached.

"Hey, Drake, c'mon over."

He faltered, thought of Wendall's bloody face, Chuck's moans, Sheri's blackened skeleton, and ran on.

"Hey, Drake, you queer or what?"

If you stop, dope, something will happen to her. She'll die. That snake—of course there's a snake in there, what the hell else can it be—will bite her and the poison will bloat her up and she'll turn black and purple and blow up all over you and it'll be all your fault because you stopped to listen.

She leaned over as he drew even with the stage. Her breasts beneath the gauze larger than he'd imagined, even though, when he had finally realized she was growing up, the eldest of the Firth children, he had also realized she had become a woman as well. The revelation had startled him, unnerved him, and the last time they had come to town, he'd done his best to avoid being alone with her. Their usual mutual teasing had suddenly developed overtones that made him uncomfortable, because he wasn't supposed to think about such things, not with or about a cousin, the daughter of his mother's sister. It was sinful. It was perverse. Deena knew it somehow, told him she did with a look and a touch, and immediately began taunting him so blatantly, so outrageously flagrantly, even her father had caught on and had yelled so furiously his face had turned red.

Red.

Blood red.

But the taunting hadn't stopped; it had merely withdrawn to become part of an occasional ambush when the grown-ups weren't looking.

"Oh . . . Drake?"

He stopped.

Even if she hadn't been there, he wouldn't have stopped. His lungs were working too hard, his legs had lost their momentum, and he could feel pressurized heat rising through his chest and face from the demands he had made. But he didn't look. He clamped his hands on his waist, closed his eyes, and concentrated on regulating his breathing, willing the aches to fade, willing his muscles not to yield and let him fall.

Deena giggled.

He swallowed, spat dryly, and would have cheerfully sold his soul for a gallon or nine of water.

"You want to see something gross?"

"No," he managed, licked his lips, licked them again.

A cat howled behind him.

Spinning around made him totter, and he grabbed the edge of the stage, lowered his head between his arms.

"Swear to god, Drake, it's really disgusting, you'll love it. Maybe you can write a story about it for the paper."

"Forget it."

She stood directly in front of him. Without raising his head he could see her tanned feet, the crimson polish on her toenails, the tiny silver bells coiled around her ankles; when she stepped closer, he could hear the carousel's song.

"C'mon, Drake, don't be a pussy."

Any minute now he'd have the strength to leave.

Any minute.

She crouched, bounced a few times before finding her balance, then lay a hand on his head. "You don't think this is the neatest thing in the world, Drake, I'll never bother you again."

Blowing his breath out now, slowly, carefully, he let himself look up, between her legs, the folds of her stomach, her breasts, her face.

She grinned.

Her teeth were black behind the veil.

"Damn, but you're going to shit when you see this."

Before he could say anything, she reached into the basket and pulled out Barbi's head, dangling it before his eyes by the short ponytail his cousin always wore because, she'd once explained, by exposing her ears it made her face seem more thin.

"Gross, am I right?"

"Wax," he said. Numb; he was numb. He had to be. Otherwise, he would have screamed.

"Like shit," she snapped, and raked a fingernail across a cheek and pointed at the blood that flowed brightly to the stage.

He snatched his hands away.

She dropped the head back into its basket, folded her arms over her thighs, hands dangling between, and said, "So now what do we do?"

He staggered away.

"Hey!" she called.

"I'm going home," he answered.

"What am I, suddenly ugly or something?"

"I'm going home!"

"Big shot college man, you think you're too good for me or something?"

A disgusted wave of his arm.

"Hey, reporter, you fucking forgot something, you ass!"

Something hit him hard on the lower back. Angrily he turned, and saw Barbi's head roll to a stop on the ground, bleeding from the gouge Deena had torn in her cheek, one eye open, the other eye puffed closed, the forked tongue of a dead snake protruding between her lips.

He felt the impact again, flinched, and tore off his shirt, threw it aside.

Deena whistled and applauded from the stage.

Kill her, he thought; what the hell, you're probably dead anyway, so go over there and kill the bitch, why the hell not.

She jeered.

He flexed his fingers, rolled his shoulders, and glared as she jumped up and down on the stage, tearing off her veil, her top, grabbing her breasts and pointing them at him, sneering, calling him names, turning around and yanking down the harem pants, spreading her legs and looking at him upside down.

He started for her.

She laughed, fell into a somersault and came up facing him, hugging her knees and winking.

Kill her; sonofabitch, I'll kill her.

Close enough to see the basket, close enough to know there was something else inside.

Deena sobered and stood up, arms crossed over her chest.

Close enough to see the weave of the straw.

"Drake?"

She was frightened.

He grinned.

"Drake, you're not going to hurt me, are you?"

He had it now. He had it.

Her arms fell away slowly.

"Don't hurt me, Drake. Be nice. Don't hurt me."

But she didn't move away.

He knew why.

He was in control.

Perhaps subconsciously before, but definitely consciously now. He was in control, and whatever he did to Deena he would do of his own choice.

The cobra lashed out of the basket before he could react. It struck her in the stomach, dropped, rose, struck her again on the hip.

She screamed.

He stopped.

Skin turning black, turning purple, turning a hideous yellow; splitting and spitting blood.

Damn, he thought, and turned away.

"If you don't stop," she said, "I'm going to break you in half."

He kept walking toward the exit, elbowing aside a young man swaggering along with his girl.

"Damnit, Drake!"

Jill tried to grab his shoulder, but he shrugged the hand away. "I gotta get home, okay?" he said, not caring if she heard him. His choice this time, not hers.

"Drake, you're nuts!" From her voice, she wasn't following.

He waved her a good-bye and passed under the arch, crossed Mainland Road and headed for home. The music softened behind him. The voice of the crowd became a murmur. The wind kicked at him and he kicked back, sending a stone into the street.

Dark houses.

He didn't care.

This weekend would be one his aunt and uncle would never forget. One word, one cockeyed look, and he'd let them know what he'd been thinking for the past ten years. His mother would be furious, but he'd feel great. As long as, he reminded himself, he held onto his resolve. And to do that, all he had to do was remember what he'd done, what he had cause to have done, to Wendall and Chuck and Deena and the others. How it happened didn't matter. Dreams, wish fulfillment, side-stepping into a world where he wasn't so thoughtful after all—it didn't matter. The guilt and the fear were gone, replaced by something still under experimentation. As of now it had no taste, but when he was finished he knew it would taste sweet.

A snake hissed in the gutter.

He stepped off the curb and walked on.

Tomorrow—maybe—he'd call Jill to apologize. Not humble himself. Just apologize. If she wanted more, she'd have to wait, and wait a long time.

A shadow stalked him across darkened lawns. At the corner, he whirled and drew his gun, fired, heard the scream, and walked on.

And tomorrow—definitely—he'd go to the newspaper and suggest to the editor that he was a little tired of writing paragraphs about birthday parties and high school awards. Even in the Station, damnit, there were more important things than that. How the hell, he would say, am I going to learn about the news if I don't get to do anything about it?

If the editor complained, he would walk out, what the hell.

And if his mother complained, he would tell her that he loved her, and she should mind her own business, that he had his own map now and finally knew how to read it.

A waltz played on a harpsicord.

He clapped his hands impatiently.

The music stopped.

"Make love to me, Drake," a woman asked from behind a hedge.

"Put your clothes on," he answered without breaking stride. "Ask me again tomorrow."

At the last corner, his corner, he stopped and clasped his hands, placed them against his lips and stared up block.

No lights.

No movement.

An automobile parked in front of his house.

A brief moment of panic—damn, they're here already; shit, I'm in trouble—before he lowered his hands to his pockets, squared his shoulders. And moved on, slowing in puzzlement when he recognized his mother's car, and there was none in the drive.

So they weren't here yet.

Despite his resolution he couldn't help the relief, pleased he wouldn't have to display his excuses.

Halfway up the walk he saw her on the porch.

"Hi," he said.

"Where were you?"

"Didn't you read the note?"

"I've been home for over an hour, Drake. I had hoped you'd be here."

At the bottom of the steps he stopped, rubbed the back of his neck, and hoped she saw his apologetic smile. "I went a little nuts," he explained. "I did everything—did you see the steaks in the fridge?—and couldn't sit anymore." He heard the whining, couldn't help it. "I wasn't gone for more than a couple of hours." A deep breath. "C'mon, Mom, what's the big deal?"

"The big deal," she said, voice tight, "is that if you had been here like you were supposed to be, I wouldn't have had to wait to tell you."

Control, he ordered; don't lose it now.

"Mom—"

"They're dead."

His laugh was short. "What?"

"They're dead."

Up a step. She backed away toward the door.

"Mom, what the hell are you talking about? Who's dead?"

"Wendall," she said flatly. "Sheri. The kids."

The second step, although his legs felt like wood.

"The state police said—"

"State police?"

"—they had apparently gotten the car fixed—"

"Mom, what are—"

She stamped her foot. "Do not. Interrupt. Me."

Third step, with palms slick and a hint of ice on his back.

Dead? Deena and Barbi?

His mother a black ghost beside the screen door, features faint, still in the blouse and skirt she had worn to work that morning.

"They were nearly to Harley when a truck—a milk truck, for god's sake—swerved over the center line. Wendall tried to avoid it, but he was speeding—trying to get here, obviously—and clipped the truck and hit a tree."

Not a dream; not a dreamer.

"Oh Jesus, Mom."

A cricket relieved the silence, soon followed by one tree frog calling to another.

"Come up here."

It's all right, he told himself; this doesn't change anything. You've still got control now. You're just going to have to help her through this. Later; you can tell her later.

On the porch he let her take his left hand; hers was dry, parchment, as if she suffered a high fever.

"You have no idea," she said quietly, her voice breaking, "how long I've waited."

"Mom, please, it wasn't—"

She opened the screen door and propped it with one foot. The inner door was already ajar. "Years. It seems like a hundred."

"Years?" This was getting too much. "Mom, if it was more than two hours, I'll eat Mr. Tarman's glider."

She reached over her head and smacked the beveled globe,

smacked it again until the night-light came on. Then she stepped inside, pulling him toward her. He resisted, thinking maybe she was a little crazy with grief. When she pulled again, however, he obeyed.

And stopped.

"Years," she repeated wearily, and snapped her fingers. The kitchen light came on. "I never thought it would happen."

He couldn't move.

"What? What would happen?"

Another snap; a lamp in the living room showed him her face. She was grinning, with tears in her eyes.

"You know," she said, and laughed without a sound. "You saw it."

He couldn't move.

"Mom?"

"They picked at me," she said bitterly, still smiling. "Like I was a chicken bone, leftover turkey. They picked me to death, and they wouldn't stop." A hand reached into the light and touched his chest, brushed it, pulled away. "He went away, the bastard, and they swooped in like vultures. They sat on me. They picked. Rene's the baby, Wendall, she doesn't know what she's doing." Her eyes closed. "I swear to God, Drake, I don't know what I would have done if it hadn't come back."

He couldn't move, could scarcely breathe.

She winked. "I took a ride, dear. Just like you did. On Tuesday, remember? He took me to the fair."

Oh Jesus oh God.

"And you," she said, "thought it was you, didn't you?"

Couldn't move.

Wanted to scream.

"Darling," she said, almost crooning, "I'm your mother, sweetheart, I'm not stupid. And don't look at me like that, dear.

Don't think you're going to get away before I decide it's time."
The hand again, patting his chest, dusting it, pinching it once.
Hard. "Think about it. Stand there a little while and think
about it." Her face hardened, became sharp, inhuman. "I have
quite an imagination, Drake. Don't believe for a minute I can't
lose you too if it means losing control."

She walked away slowly, humming, running a finger over
the newel post as she headed for the kitchen.

Her shadow on the floor was of a woman, dancing; her
shadow on the wall was cobra spreading its hood; the figure
passing through the doorway was a vulture settling its wings.

He tried to move, tried to call her, but he was trapped and
he knew it, and knew there was nothing he could do as long as
he was lost in the amber light.

His mother knew it too.

She knew him as well, had shaped him and trained him and
made certain that he wouldn't turn out like his father; she
had loved him and nursed him and encased him in debt swad-
dled in devotion; she had educated and disciplined and di-
rected and loved.

The sun rose.

Jill came looking for him, and was told that he had gone off
with some friends first thing that morning and wouldn't be
back until nightfall.

Kayman Kalb came looking for work, and was set to
sweeping the porch and sidewalk, trimming the edges of the
lawn, sitting with his mother on the porch swing and eating a
sandwich before leaving.

The sun set.

The air cooled.

Jill didn't return.

And Drake, far from lost in the amber light, didn't panic, simply waited.

Tonight.

Tomorrow.

It didn't matter.

The bulb would burn out or loosen in its socket the way it always did, the way his father had left it.

He knew where the extra bulbs were, and he had ridden the carousel, heard the music tin and silver.

All he needed was control.

She would teach him how to use it.

IV

The Rain Is Filled with Ghosts Tonight

THE LAST HOUR OF THE DEAD; THE LONG GRAVEN hour before the sun bleeds the horizon, when nothing distinguishes tree from sky, lawn from road, dreams from sitting up and screaming in the dark; when the day's weighted heat hasn't yet begun to simmer; when birds and cats and large shapeless crows stir for early hunting, when cattle in a valley barn begin to shift nervously in their stalls, when chickens in a valley coop begin to talk to one another, softly, querying, ruffling their feathers, blinking their eyes; when dark cars in dark driveways begin to grumble in preparation for a dark ride into light; when the souls that remember return to their husks, and the souls that forget can't find their way home.

In the last hour of the dead.

The house in the middle of the block between Poplar and Thorn was long and low and feeling its age. Two stories and dark green, a squat peaked roof and a pair of out-of-true chimneys, the windows with shutters nailed open, shades drawn halfway, white curtains tufted and closed. It was overhung with trees, a few branches brushing the shingles and allowing the squirrels to take shortcuts at midnight and sometimes find their way into the attic. Cedar chips scattered around flowering shrubs on the front lawn. Fat evergreen shrubs hiding the foundation.

The porch, narrow and warped to a slight cant across the width of the house, had its stairs on the left end, leading down to a path of three chipped flagstones, which in turn led to a weed-marked blacktop drive. At the top of the stairs, on either side, two potted yuccas that nearly touched the flat roof. Gingerbread around the squared posts and window frames. Ivy and dense fern in clay pots hanging from the ceiling, swinging gently, chains silent. A large brown cat, indolent, insolent, curled by the doormat. At the far end, a standing glider, rain-warped, hinge-rusted, flanked by wrought iron tables to hold ashtrays and glasses.

Four chairs, one a rocker.

After a second's consideration, Kayman settled in the one nearest the steps and with a grunt propped his slippered feet on the railing. It wasn't very comfortable considering the state of his knees, much easier when he was younger, but it was the only way he knew how to sit out here without feeling as if he were a captive in some godawful home, waiting for an officious scrawny nurse to bring a blanket for his legs and a scolding for being out. Defiantly casual, the hell with the cramps. Then: the hell with this too, what are you trying to prove, you're all alone, you old fart. But he waited a long second before lowering his legs, then pulled the chair forward and folded his hands across his stomach. Better; much better. This way he could see Northland Avenue without having to squint between his feet. Not that there was anything to see this time of day, but it was the principle that mattered, and the fact that he was ready.

He was a large man still, though his arms showed signs of shrinking, and over the past two years he'd let his hair grow to his shoulders. The young men stared with amusement, the young women sometimes shook their heads in pity, but he didn't mind the reaction as long as they didn't laugh in his face.

This far along, he figured he'd earned the right to do what he wanted, look how he wanted, sit all damn day if he wanted without being scolded.

Behind him, a light he sensed more than saw.

She was up.

She was always up when the space beside her was empty.

She would call him, call again, before grabbing her robe from the bedside chair and slipping it on, come down to the kitchen and stand at the stove wondering which would be better this morning, tea or cocoa. Whichever it was, it would be too hot. In the middle of a blizzard, it would always be too hot.

All right, you old jackass, he thought; all right, no need to be cranky. She does her best, she ain't a magician, y'know.

Have to be, he answered, stick with you all this time.

Begrudging smile, and a grunt.

The breath of a west wind trembled the ivy and lace-top ferns; a branch creaked, leaves pawing at the house, the panes, like the small hands of beggars; somewhere up the street, wind chimes discordant and distant enough to be a dream.

The smell of damp.

He leaned forward then, looked up from under the eaves, tried to tell from the missing stars if the cloud he had seen the night before was still there, if there would be rain today. For a change. The grass, while not dying, wouldn't last much longer; the flowers, while not wilting, would soon lose their brilliance. He could use the sprinkler the way his neighbors did, of course, in the middle of the night when they thought no one was watching, no one could hear. But they could afford the higher quarterly bills; they could pay without wincing.

Rain was what he needed.

For this, and other things.

But he could see nothing conclusive. Too many streets, and the streetlamps too bright despite their foliage cloaks. He'd have to wait until sunrise.

The cat stirred then, claws scratching across the straw welcome mat, a single thump when its tail met the wall, a single mutter when it yawned.

She was coming.

His hands, still clasped, shifted to rest beneath his chin, felt the stubbles there and rubbed across them. He had last shaved two days ago, best he could remember. Maybe today he'd strop the old razor and mow his cheeks clear, maybe not. She was the only one who would have cared, and she didn't. She kissed him anyway, wrinkling her nose and lightly boxing his ear, telling him she would pack and run away if he didn't make himself presentable, for her if not the world.

She wouldn't.

The grass grew and the cat slaughtered birds and she was always there when he woke up in the middle of the night, listening to the voices whisper under his window.

The screen door complained.

The cat arched its back and waddled to the glider, sniffed the thin cushion, jumped up, and settled with a great chorus of rusty hinges.

"This is getting to be a habit," she said, not really complaining, taking the chair beside him and settling her robe about her knees, tucking her feet back. "Maybe we could move the mattress down here, you wouldn't fall down the stairs in the middle of the night."

He nodded.

A cup nudged his arm until he took it, blew on it, sipped it. Tea, and too damn hot. Gingerly he placed it on the floor beside him before it burned through his fingers.

Wind soughing and sighing, a leaf jumping in the drive.

"Don't see why you don't put on the porch light."

"I like the dark," he told her, as he'd told her before, many times. "The light's too damn noisy this time of day."

"This time of day is for sleeping, not sitting."

Footsteps on the pavement, soft and slow.

"No. Thinking."

She chuckled. "Oh really, now. About what? You do it every morning most days anymore. What's left to think about?"

The footsteps approached the house from the right. Soft and slow. Not someone walking a dog, not someone home impossibly late from a party. Not someone heading for work, impossibly early. Someone walking. Soft and slow. Taking his time.

The rocker tipped back as a short rotund man in a wellworn tweed jacket ridiculously warm for the weather and much too tight across his shoulders sat down with a theatrical moan, pulled out a cigarette, and lit it. "The trouble with getting married, Kayman," he said, hoarse and reedy, "is that you're never alone when you want to be."

"I'm not married, Johnny."

"Oh. Of course. I forgot."

"Was once."

"I remember."

"Didn't much like it."

The cigarette winked orange. "I remember that too."

Her hand covered his on the armrest. A gentle touch. A

tender squeeze. Fingers more bone than flesh, though they couldn't be any softer. "Still thinking?"

He looked at her, had to look down, and nodded. "Like I said, Estelle."

Her face, barely visible despite of the glow from the street, was pale, more wrinkled than his, eyebrows still dark though her hair was loose and grey. Whenever she despaired and threatened a face-lift, he insisted they weren't old wrinkles, they were character wrinkles. He was partly right. If she lived another thirty years she would never be ancient.

"They called again yesterday, you know," she said, squeezing again, easing off. "While you were at the hardware store, yelling at poor Mayard."

"Wasn't yelling," he insisted. "Damn fool sold me shoddy goods. Can't do my work if he sells me shoddy goods."

"You whack at the cat with a yardstick, dear, and you hit a tree, it's going to break. That isn't shoddy, that's dumb."

"Yeah, well . . ." He pulled a handkerchief from his pocket and blew his nose loudly. "He gave me another one."

"Because he's a good man."

A band of cigarette smoke floated over the railing, shredding slowly.

A slight shift in the breeze and he caught the perpetual smell of sawdust that clung to his clothes, his skin, residue of his cabinetry, the work he had done, and done well, since leaving the office several decades ago. His avocation had become, overnight, his vocation. It also supplemented the government checks that weren't large enough to feed a sparrow. He inhaled, and smiled to himself; his sawdust and Estelle's perfumed soap, what a combination.

He looked back to the street, listening to the footsteps taking their time arriving. "They called, huh?"

She nodded, fussing with the cloth belt of her robe. "Right after Flory did. She wanted to know if we'd have dinner with her this weekend. I said it was all right."

He grunted.

"Then," she said, "it was them. Not two seconds later. I didn't even have time to take a breath. I didn't want to tell you. You'd only get mad."

"Damn right."

"But I can't sleep when they get like that. Kayman, what if they take me?"

"Worrying," he said, turning his hand over, clasping hers, "is my job, remember? It was our deal. Yours is to keep me from attacking the ladies."

Her smile was one-sided. "Not much to worry about there anymore."

"Oh, you think so?"

Her free hand brushed across his cheeks, under his chin, patted the side of his neck. "Wearing a hedgehog like that, they won't come near you."

The footsteps paused.

"Hedgehogs," he said haughtily, "are mighty damn cute."

The footsteps moved on.

"And damnit, how many times have I told you, they aren't going to take you if you don't want to go."

He couldn't see who it was.

"What are you frowning at?" she asked.

"Trying to see who's out there this time of morning. Crazy time for exercise. Be dead before they're forty."

The hand slipped away.

He closed his eyes briefly: oh hell.

"Kayman."

"Okay, all right."

She always got like this—distant and close to whimpering—when she couldn't see what he saw, hear what he heard. Her eyes were worse than his, but she wore her glasses only when she cooked or watched television; his eyes, touch wood, had never needed a day's correction in his life. Never would. He was old, just a spit the other side of seventy-five; but he damn sure wasn't feeble.

"Kayman, please don't do that again. It scares me."

"I forgot. I'm sorry."

"Promise me."

"Promise."

The cigarette drew an orange rectangle in the dark.

Kayman reached down for his tea, drank it and wished to hell she'd forget about what all the doctors said and give him sugar once in a while, this tasted like colored water, then handed her the cup. "Think maybe you'd better get some rest."

She shook her head. Yawned. Laughed.

"See?"

"All right," she said.

He stood, helped her up, put an arm around her waist and walked her back to the door. Hugged her, kissed the top of her head. "Sleep in. You need it."

Her lips moved against his chest, a palm patted his hip, and she was gone.

" 'Night, Estelle," Johnny called.

Kayman watched her through the screen, watched her pause at the foot of the stairs before using the bannister to pull herself up. One step at a slow time. Head bent, right arm angled away from her side for balance. Stopping. Looking up. Climbing. Her new hip giving her trouble again. That, and other things.

Goddamn, you die on me, Estelle, he thought to her back, suddenly angry, you'll kill me.

The cat leapt off the glider, the shriek of the chains spinning Kayman around, right hand in a fist, eyes narrow as he searched the porch, the yard he could see, for intruders, invaders, his breath quick and shallow, heat flushing through his cheeks until, with a relieved gasp, he sagged against the wall and wiped his face with his forearm.

"Jumpy," Johnny said. A dark-spotted hand patted down gleaming, stiff black hair. "Nerves like that will put you in your grave."

"Shut up."

"It's my curse: my tongue."

"Shut up anyway."

"If you like."

Hands deep in his pockets, he left the porch and walked down the drive. At the sidewalk he made another check of the sky, and despite his hope there'd be showers later, for his grass and flowers, he really didn't want them. The rain bothered him. It did too many things it wasn't supposed to do; some days it made him believe he was losing his mind, one thought at a time, and since the beginning of summer it had been getting progressively worse. The concrete's chill seeped up through his slippers and locked his knees. Down the street, toward Thorn Road, headlamps blared and an engine raced at the curb.

A glance down, and he spotted his shadow and relaxed, took a deep cleansing breath, and decided to take a quick nap on the couch before breakfast.

The sun was on its way.

The clouds he spotted were thin and shapeless, more a haze than a cover.

Back on the porch, he pulled the chairs away from the railing, scratched the cat behind its ears until it granted him a purring, took hold of one of the glider's chains and squinted at the hooks buried in the ceiling. Oil, he decided; a little oil later will stop all that racket. Get the stepladder, listen to Estelle worry about his falling, squirt some oil up there, over here, it'll be silent as a ghost.

You too, he warned the screen door when it opened loudly; your days are numbered, you squeaky son of a bitch; and when it slammed shut behind him, its spring too taut, he kicked at it, stalked into the living room and stood in the middle of the floor, seeing none of the books on their shelves, none of the magazines in their cradle by her armchair, none of the framed photographs on the bare oak mantel. He saw his reflection instead. Head and neck on the wall over the sofa.

He recognized the face well enough; he didn't recognize the expression. Like a child whose favorite toy had just broken, and he didn't understand why, and didn't yet want to cry; like a young man whose girl had just walked out of the room, head up, hips swinging, elbows angrily tight to her sides, and he didn't know why, and didn't yet want to cry; like a man who watched at the site of a grave while a rumbling machine made of greasy cogs and strips of dark green canvas lowered a coffin into a hole, bearing flowers and brass, and he didn't understand, and didn't yet want to cry.

No; not true.

Not true at all.

He dropped heavily onto the center cushion, sat there a short while before letting himself slowly topple over. Legs up, slippers kicked off toe to heel, one hand under his cheek, the other dangling over.

Maybe, he thought, half in a doze, if I sleep all day it will all go away.

It wouldn't, though.

It hadn't yet, even when he'd tried it.

Walking hadn't worked either, to the park and around it on the inside, to the Cock's Crow and a few beers before walking home again, to the depot out on Cross Valley Road to watch the trains and listen to the passengers and gossip with the stationmaster before walking back.

None of it had worked.

None of it had stopped the world from twisting slightly out of shape.

And none of it had explained why it had started.

"It's like," he said to Flory Sholcroft just a tick past noon, "there's this big pot, you see, and I'm sort of treading water in the middle or standing on something I can't see, and then someone comes along with this damn ladle or spoon or stick or something and starts stirring the damn thing. Not a lot, you understand. It's like when you give the soup a quick stir to keep it from burning, you see? Things start moving around, but I don't, and . . ." He spread his hands away from his plate, then picked up a fork and jabbed at a piece of his steak. "Estelle thinks it's her." He chewed and swallowed. "I haven't told her it's me."

"Merry-go-round," Flory said, long, red-tipped fingers darting over her plate to rearrange her hamburger, her french fries, the two leaves of lettuce on which had died a slice of tomato.

"What?"

"I think merry-go-round is a better image." She grinned as she touched the corner of her mouth with a napkin. "You're riding around in circles, see, and the rest of the world stands around watching. They're there, then they're gone, then they're back but in a slightly different place, or with a different expression, or whatever."

He thought about it. "Maybe."

"All of which makes you think, merry-go-round or soup pot, that you're going nuts, right?"

He grimaced. "Hell of a way for a shrink to talk."

"Kayman, I've been talking to you like this for years, and you haven't slugged me yet. You think just because you come for a little advice in my professional capacity now and then I'm going to treat you any differently?" Before he could lean away, she reached over and gripped his arm. "You and Estelle are like my second set of parents, you great idiot. You helped me when they died, I'm doing my best to help you now. Okay?"

He supposed it was fair, but it didn't feel right.

This woman was half his age, handsome in a way most men found intimidating, strong in a way that frightened most of them off. Unlike him, she had never married. Yet she didn't look anything like a spinster, her hair still blond and flowing, figure still heart-skipping full, a face he could put his hands around and pinch and mold and squeeze until he wept. Hell of a way, he thought, for a doctor to look.

And a hell of a thing too for him to be here like this. Sneaking away from home on the pretense of a short stroll and calling Flory from the phone booth over in the corner by the kitchen entrance, telling her he'd like to talk again, it looked like rain today. Then calling Estelle and telling her he'd met some buddies and would eat at the Crow if she didn't mind, maybe walk back to the Travelers after they were done. Did she want to meet him there? They could blow the budget and have some fun, ride the carousel, see the ghost house, maybe catch the animal show he'd heard about from some of the kids in the park. She could get a cab from Bartlett's to bring her over, or maybe a neighbor to drive her. Or should he come back and pick her up?

She had answered no to it all. It was going to pour any minute, she claimed, and if he had any of the sense left that God had given him, he'd come straight home after eating. But then he didn't have any sense, did he, because he was too damn stubborn to think he'd ever catch pneumonia, much less a summer cold. So don't worry about me, I'll be fine, I've got plenty to do and none it needs you. He'd hung up much relieved; after living with her for twenty years come next September, he knew that being with Estelle in a mood like that would be like riding a witch's broomstick with the witch right behind him, seething at the world.

As he chewed his last piece of meat, he looked up at one of the wagon wheel chandeliers, and smiled to himself, remembering a time.

"You made an ass of yourself then," Johnny said, leaning over the back from the boot behind.

"Did not."

"Did so," a woman declared, poking her thin-hair head up beside Johnny. Red lips, red cheeks, bloodshot eyes, cigar mashed into a silver holder. "You took your goddamn clothes off."

God, yes, so he had.

"Claimed you were Tarzan," she continued, holder clamped between yellowed, horsey teeth. "You climbed up on a table, jumped from there and hung from one of the spokes."

"Hanging out, as it were," Johnny said, chuckling.

"Shut up," she said.

"Hey, hey, Brenda, let's not forget a lady's manners."

She jabbed him hard with a stiff finger, and he yelped, disappeared below the back, and Kayman could hear him muttering about medical expenses and lawsuits.

"You ought to leave him alone," Kayman warned her gently.

"What the hell for?"

"Because I'll leave you!" Johnny shouted.

Brenda winked. "No, he won't. He can't. He's in love."

"Hell I am!"

"Mind your own business, you fruit."

His head only to his eyes rose over the booth, eyebrows waggling. "I was banana enough for you at one time, sweetie pie."

Kayman laughed.

Brenda snapped around and vanished, smoke billowing behind to measure the strength of the insult, and the embarrassment of the truth.

Still chuckling, and remembering, he emptied his glass of milk and said to Flory, "They called again yesterday. I wasn't there, but they called."

"Who?"

"Her kids. I told you about them last time."

Flory pushed her plate to one side, nibbled on a fry. "They still don't want you two living together."

He shook his head.

"The home threat again?"

She knew about the children—Jesus, children! they were damn near fifty, both of them—and their thus-far futile attempts over the past five years to put their mother into a nursing home, down where they lived in suburban Atlanta. To protect her, they said; to expose her to a better, healthier climate, they said; to watch over her in her declining years, they had the goddamn nerve to say last Christmas when they called and refused to talk to him when he answered. And until now, Estelle had been strong enough, mother enough, to keep them in their place, slap them down, turn them around and put a sting to their nosy butts.

Then the rain began to bring things to the house.

She became afraid for her mind.

Flory touched his hand.

He didn't look while she spoke, watching instead the jukebox over behind the piano; a man stood there, bending over, reading the titles, a quarter tapping the glass face while he decided. Kayman knew him. Saw him several times up at the library, once in a while at the Brass Ring. Big fella. Skinny as hell. Keeps trying to grow a beard, but it only makes him look like a rug got at by termites not very choosy about their meals. Played darts once; the guy had lost badly.

Flory told him it wasn't right that he should let Estelle believe she was the one who missed things, because the things she thought she missed weren't really there. He knew that. Fear of what she might think was only being cruel, not to mention hugely selfish.

What was the bastard's name, he wondered, scowling in concentration. Hal? Jerry? He would use the alphabet trick— go through all the letters, the name would come when he reached the right one. Al? Artie? Benny?

"Kayman, what you're doing is wrong. You know it's wrong, and you'll have to stop it."

A fist rested on the table, knuckles bleeding white.

This was crazy. How the hell could he forget the name of a guy he saw only yesterday, for Christ's sake? Carl? Danny? Ed?

The man made his selection, turned around, and as he walked back to his table, saw Kayman and waved.

Kayman returned the wave with a nod.

Johnny and Brenda began to dance by the bar at the back of the room.

Jesus Christ, what the hell was his name?

Something bounced off his chest.

He looked down at his plate and saw a french fry skid across and off it. The fist mashed it. The plate bounced. His empty glass toppled over, and she caught it before it rolled off the table onto the floor.

When he glared, he could see how hard she tried to stay unmoved.

"If," he said, leaning over, voice low and deep, "she thinks I'm crazy, she'll leave me."

"No."

"If," he said, feeling the plate's edge press into his stomach, "she thinks I'm crazy, she'll leave me."

"She won't, Kayman, I promise. You just say the word, and I'll come over and help you. It won't be easy, but for Estelle's sake, you can't keep this up."

"They do not," he said, slapping the plate off the table and ignoring the crash, "leave me."

Her lips quivered in indignation, stopped, and she picked up her purse. "Well I am, Kayman. Right now." She slid out of the booth, purse stiff against her waist. "When you've calmed down, give me a call."

She left ahead of the gunshots of her heels.

He stared at the back of the seat opposite him, paying no attention to the busboy sweeping up the pieces, not listening to the song the man had selected, not blinking when a woman slid into the booth and folded her hands on the table.

She was thin, not pretty and not plain, ordinary and wearing an ordinary light summer dress with puffed sleeves and tiny blue flowers somewhat faded from constant washing. Short brown hair that had always caught the sun in hints of red. Chestnut, she claimed; he didn't call it anything but brown. A rounded chin age promised to point. Dark hazel eyes that didn't look away when he leaned back and sighed loudly and used his left hand to force open the fist. She didn't blink. Her expression was blank, as if she were looking right through him, thinking about something else, something unimportant, something automatic, like shopping or making love.

He knew the look.

He knew the woman.

He fumbled out his wallet, looked at the check, and dropped a bill over it.

She didn't move.

He grabbed a french fry from Flory's plate and jammed it into his mouth as he pushed out of the booth.

She didn't move.

A step away, a step back; he leaned over the table and said, "Changed my mind, get the hell away."

She didn't move.

When he left, yanking the door open and looking back with a scowl because he didn't want to, she was still there, and Johnny and Brenda were still there as well, slow dancing alone in the middle of the floor.

He didn't go to the carnival. The sight of all those people crowding around at the entrance, a sign tacked to the arch telling them only a few days left, soured his mood further, so he went to the library instead, read and didn't see the words, flipped through magazines and didn't see the pictures, finally went to the park where he sat by the pond. Beneath a tree. Flipping pebbles into the water.

Tears made an effort, but he shook them back, not really knowing why. He *should* cry, damnit. Hell, he had a *right* to cry. He had just turned away by his own stupidity one of the few friends he had left who could still do him some good. Flory was a saint and he had goddamn stoned her.

A fist pressed to his brow, the other one smacking his knee.

Why was it so hard anymore?

After all these years, it ought to get easier; it sure ought to get simpler.

Why was it so hard?

Johnny used to talk about paying your dues. You learned, you worked hard, with your own two hands you built your reputation, it didn't matter where, and these were your dues. So Jesus Christ, hadn't he paid enough? Would he still be paying when they dropped him in his grave?

"That's not right," his wife had told him, back there at the house so long ago, before she'd tried to leave. "You think that, it means you figure the world owes you just because you're alive."

"No, Ronnie, that's wrong."

Nearly a head shorter than he, thin despite all the food she put away, chestnut hair more often than not wrapped in a red net so the wind wouldn't ruin what she'd taken all day to put together. Which wasn't, by then, one hell of a lot.

"It's right," she insisted, and picked a speck of tobacco off her lower lip. "Johnny's talking through his hat. Dues don't exist except for those who need excuses."

"Oh?" He had been a real smartass back then, carrying a leather briefcase, wearing three-piece pin-striped suits and shoes shined every morning, working with figures, making people money in a brokerage firm on Centre Street. "Then what does?"

She had never really understood, had never quite been able to grasp the fact that the figures he brought home with him weren't related in any way to the figures on his paycheck; not understanding when he tried to explain that the numbers he talked about weren't his numbers at all.

They got by.

"C'mon, Ronnie, if I don't have to pay my dues so we can have some economic security and we won't have to starve in our old age, what the hell does exist, huh?"

For the first time in years, her face softened despite the fact that he'd ended up shouting, and behind the pale lipstick, the eye shadow, the blush, he saw her the way she was when she wasn't being Mrs. Kalb—eyes to sleep sweetly in, a smile to lie gently in, a way of stroking the back of his hand the way she crooned to the children when they were babies and sick.

But somewhere along the line, somewhere back there in the late payment of bills and the deals made with creditors and the time they had nearly lost the car to the bank, that woman began to sink and the other one had emerged. It didn't make any difference that no store, no credit card, no lender, had ever been cheated; it didn't matter that eventually everyone got their cup of his blood. She sank. She surfaced.

Ronnie died.

Ronnie was born.

"You going to tell me or are you just going to stand there like a lump?"

She stubbed the cigarette out in a saucer on the kitchen counter and leaned back, palm to her chin, elbow cradled in her other hand.

"Hanging on," she said at last. A shrug. "What the hell else can you do?"

"You could pull yourself up."

A smile sweet and sour: "To do that, you'd have to let go."

Right, he thought bitterly as he watched a pair of squirrels chase each other around the pond, scaring the ducks into the middle, making a couple of kids on the other side roar with laughter; right.

So he worked harder, made more money, and the day after he turned forty, she left him.

Or at least, he thought with grim satisfaction, she gave it a good try.

The squirrels paused in front of him, tails up and quivering. Then one bolted and the other followed, and he heard them soon after climbing the tree at his back, chattering, scrabbling, chattering again.

The water darkened.

He peered through the branches, shading his eyes; the overcast had thickened.

Oh lord, he thought, licking his lips nervously; oh lord, it's gonna rain.

In the last hour of the dead, he stood alone on the porch, fully dressed. The sky was still cloudy, the wind still damp, the cat crouched on the glider and growling low in its throat as shadows drifted across the lawn, wove dark patterns between the flowers, approached but did not come near the unlighted house. They never came near. They were never allowed.

He watched them without expression. Not shadows at all, not really; disturbances of the air that made things slowly turn, that made things shift, that confused and blurred vision until shapes were created, and forms, and figures.

Not shadows at all.

I tried, he thought dejectedly, knowing they would listen; a hundred times I tried to explain, but this time Flory got mad.

My fault, I suppose, but she didn't have to walk out. Damn woman. Thinks she's so goddamn smart, got all that education, read all them books, thinks she knows more than I do about what I know, figures she can put a baby bandage on it and kiss it and make it better and it will all go away, but she doesn't know anything, Jesus Christ, she don't know and she damn well won't bother to listen because what the hell, I'm an old man, right?, I don't know shit from shinola, I'm losing my grip, I got that disease whatever the hell you call it, it rots your brain so you can't even shit by yourself anymore, can't remember your kid's name, so why should she pay attention to someone like me when someone like me don't even know what's going on in the world, not like her, not like her books, hell, no, she's just too good, been screwing around with me all this time, probably writing one of those paper things shrinks gotta write to get famous or rich or get a promotion or whatever it is she'll get from pretending all this time she was my friend, I'm her goddamn second father and she probably left him too, probably left him lying in a hospital dying of one damn thing or another, calling for her while she's out telling other people how to run their lives with fancy words that ain't nothing but damn good common sense.

The hell with it.

The wind strengthened.

He checked the dining room window, but he didn't see any light. She hadn't woken up, she hadn't come down, she was still asleep up there all alone while he was down here, talking to his damn self and trying to hold on. Hold on. That's all he had to do until her goddamn kids finally saw the goddamn light. Hold on. Then they'd go away and she wouldn't think he was crazy.

But at least it wasn't raining.

192 | CHARLES GRANT

At least the shapes and forms and figures out there weren't even shadows.

Count your lucky stars, Kayman old boy, count your lucky stars even if you can't see them.

That afternoon, Estelle decided to go to the market to get some things for the larder. He knew she really didn't need to, there was plenty to eat in the cupboards and the fridge, but he had stuck around the house all day, feeling guilty about his meeting with Flory, wanting to do something to atone. But there was nothing to do. The screens had all been patched where needed, the back stoop repaired, the lawn mowed just a few days ago, the garage cleaned out the week before—the easiest job these days since they no longer had a car. So he followed her, making her laugh at his earnest pleas for work, making her impatient when he tried to do her chores as well.

"That does it," she announced in exasperation when he asked, practically begged, if he could help clean the silverware. "You're driving me nuts. I'm going to the store."

"Good idea," he agreed. "I'll go with you."

Immediately, her hand slapped and clung to his chest. "You can go, but you can't stay with me or I'll probably end up braining you with a pork chop."

"Okay." He held up his hands. "Okay, no problem."

As he hurried upstairs to brush his hair and shave, he caught a glimpse of her expression, and it almost changed his mind. She was still worried. But it wasn't about herself. Him. It was about him. He knew that look, knew it as well as he knew the touch of her lips. He had seen it for nearly twenty years— whenever he was ill, whenever he injured himself doing carpentry or plumbing, whenever he slept too long or didn't sleep enough or ate too many antacids or too many aspirins. He knew that look, and in knowing it knew that sometime that morning, Flory must have called and told her everything.

He cut himself shaving, the first time in a decade.

For the first time in a decade he didn't check the hairs left in the brush.

"Hon, are you okay?" she called from the foyer.

Eyes closed, hands gripping the edge of the sink, feet well apart, breathing in, breathing out, shaping his rage into something he could handle.

"Down in a minute. Gotta make myself beautiful."

"Damnit, Kay, I'm an old woman, I haven't got the time."

In spite of himself, he chuckled, laughed, practically skipped out of the bathroom and down the stairs. Grabbed her in his arms and kissed her. Kissed her again when she gasped and stared in amazement.

"What . . . ?"

"Ask me no questions," he said, leading her out the door, "I'll tell you no lies."

"When pigs fly," she said, and waved when a car honked at the curb.

He stiffened.

"Kayman," she said, voice low and warning. "My hip's giving me trouble today. The rain coming, I guess. So I called Norma for a ride. Don't you dare say a word."

That was an easy promise, and he gave it with as much good grace as he could manage. It was hard, though; lord, it was hard. Norma Hobbs, for a schoolteacher, was about the most unpleasant woman he had ever met in his life. She lived two houses down, by herself, and had been alone since her husband died, in his twenties, of cancer. To be honest, he wasn't so sure about that; he figured it was her vinegary temper that had really done him in, and the tart sting of her tongue. He pitied the children who were stuck in her class.

Yet she was fine with Estelle. Wonderful, in fact, and for that reason, if no other, he tolerated her presence.

"Big of you," Johnny said. He sat in the backseat with him, blowing smoke out the window behind Norma's head.

"Shut up," Kayman grumbled. He was in no mood for chatter.

"And the horse you rode in on," Johnny replied, pouting. He fussed with his tweed jacket. "I just wanted to tell you something, that's all."

"Don't want to hear it."

The silence made him turn.

Johnny stared out the window, rocking easily as the car took the first corner and they passed the hospital.

Kayman rubbed his hands together.

This wasn't right.

Never, ever, was Johnny at a loss for words; and never, ever, had he offered any information. He came, alone or with Brenda, and they argued and laughed and bickered and remembered. It was a routine. It was right.

This wasn't.

"What?" he asked softly. "Johnny, I'm sorry. What?"

Johnny's head swiveled around slowly.

"Damn," Norma said, "I think it's starting to rain."

"Just spitting a little," said Estelle. "It'll make your hair grow."

The teacher chuckled.

"What, Johnny?"

"They came," he said at last.

Kayman frowned. "What? Who came?"

The cigarette pointed at the drops of water skidding along the window. "They did."

"Johnny, you're not making sense."

A teardrop in Johnny's right eye, shimmering, growing, became a raindrop on the glass that slipped out of sight.

Kayman reached out, passed a hand through the place where his best friend had been. "Johnny?"

A hand touched his shoulder, and he yelped, threw himself back in the seat, a hand before his face as if warding off a curse.

"Kayman!"

He blinked, felt his heart try to leap from his chest, and stared through the window. "I'm okay," he said.

"You most certainly are not."

"You startled me."

"You were talking to yourself," Norma said, maneuvering into the parking lot behind the theater. "Gotta watch that stuff, Kayman, they'll take you away and Estelle will have to move in with me."

"Kayman?"

He looked without turning his head. "I'm okay, I said." Looked away. People on the sidewalk, no umbrellas yet, none of the cars using their wipers. When the car stopped, Estelle immediately got out, pulled up the seat back, and leaned in. Pale. Frightened eyes, don't-leave-me-alone eyes.

A smile and wink only meant to be reassuring, only made her suspicious. He winked again and pushed forward until she had to give way. Once on his feet he gave her shoulders a quick hug and told her not to spend them into oblivion, they weren't exactly laying in for a blizzard.

Norma led her away, chatting rapidly, clearly not concerned about his health or state of mind.

Estelle looked back once, just before they crossed the street.

When a van passed between them, he put a hand on the car roof to brace himself.

they came

All right, he thought; all right, it's all right, he's just mad you snapped at him, he'll be back. They always came back. Not all at one time, though. Not even in groups. But they came, some more than others, the rest of them waiting until he wanted to talk. So what did Johnny mean? Of course they came.

One or two at a time.

His face dampened from the drizzle, and he wiped it off hard, crossed Chancellor Avenue and walked up toward the Brass Ring. It wasn't too early. A drink would calm him down. Maybe Brenda would be there. Johnny, too. A shudder that made some of the pedestrians glance at him, look away. Ronnie wouldn't be there. At the Crow yesterday was the first time he'd seen her in over a year. He seldom wanted to. She never spoke, never told him how she was. She wouldn't be there.

God, he hoped she wouldn't be there.

She wasn't.

A sparse crowd, a few at the bar, a few at the tables in back watching a lackluster game of darts. He chose the bar, the stool closest to the wall and near the door. Nigel didn't ask; he brought over a glass of beer, gave him a nod, moved away. Kayman drank slowly, and slowly dammed the panic he'd felt flooding the car. The air-conditioning helped, lifting the muggy heat from his back, raising gooseflesh on his arms until he rubbed it away. Then he let himself look around, as he twisted until he could lean against the wall. The bar was a square horseshoe, and around the corner, two stools down, a tall man in a white shirt, his jacket folded over the brass rail, lifted his empty glass for Nigel to refill. It was the man in the Cock's Crow.

Kayman grinned—it was Teddy Tarman from up on Devon Street, near the graveyard. A lot older than when seen from a distance, but not nearly as old as he. An electrician who had once helped Kayman rewire the house, asking in return nothing but a new dining table Kayman had been pleased to make, and pleased to note, on a visit not too long ago, how well the man had tended it over the years.

"On me," he told Nigel when the refill was brought.

"Thanks," Tarman said. "What's the occasion?"

"Feeling good, that's all."

"Ain't gonna argue."

They talked baseball for a while, about the football training camps and how the new kids seemed to be, this and that and eventually speculated on the whereabouts of Casey Bethune, who had evidently flown the coop a couple of weeks ago. Rumor claimed murder and illicit sex, but rumor, Kayman claimed, was more bloodthirsty than real life. Tarman laughed, agreed, and grabbed his jacket. A thanks for the beer, a call to Nigel, and he was gone.

Kayman's smile died.

Teddy Tarman.

Why the hell hadn't he remembered the name before? Or the face? Anything?

Swallow your pride, he ordered; don't be a fool, swallow your pride.

Before he lost his nerve, he paid for the drinks and hastened outside, paused when the heat grabbed him again, then walked quickly up to High Street, turned the corner, and stopped at a doorway between the piano shop and a clothing store. He'd never been here in all this time. Usually he met Flory in the park or at the Crow, a couple of times in the Brass Ring. But never in her office. What if she had a patient and couldn't talk to him? What if she didn't have a patient and still wouldn't talk?

He'd leave a note.

All he wanted was to offer an apology.

Oh lord, he thought as he reached for the knob; oh lord.

The door was locked.

He tried it again, shaded his eyes and peered in, but all he could see were the stairs leading up, blending into dark before they reached the landing. There was no note, no explanation. He stepped back to the curb and looked up at her window, hoping to find a clue. And in finding none slapped his hands uselessly against his legs and walked off, away from Centre Street, not wanting to think and unable to stop it—Estelle and Ronnie, the day the office had let him go because they were cutting back and he wasn't a senior man in spite of all his time, the day he had sold his first piece of furniture—a small foyer table in the style of Queen Anne, the way people began leaving him once he started getting old.

"They do that, you know," Brenda said, falling in step beside him.

He knew.

"They figure you've done your time."

He knew that too.

Reach a certain time, the mind and the body and the will must go. *Must* go. As if it were a law. It didn't matter the age, either; when they didn't want you, didn't believe they needed you, it didn't matter.

Grey hair.

Liver spots.

A slight stoop at the shoulders when gravity suggested you'd been born too damn tall.

Twinge in the joints even when the weather's good.

Here's your hat, Kayman, what's your hurry.

He glanced across the street, to a house tucked beneath large maples. Something was there, on the lawn. As the drizzle became a light shower, hissing carefully through the leaves, something was there.

Someone.

"What the hell is that?" he demanded when he stopped.

No answer.

Brenda was gone.

But it was there, and there was one on the sidewalk, near the last corner. Shimmering as the rain passed through it and, at the same time, giving it vague shape.

A dark figure, but not black; transparent enough to see the people hurrying now down Centre Street, but substantial enough to make its presence known.

He backed away, turned, and saw another one on the corner across the road.

Standing there.

Just . . . standing.

they came

Short quick breaths then as he tried to decide how much of it was real, how much simple distortions in the air.

Another one, behind a low hedge.

Standing.

He hurried, wanted to run, felt his legs crying for a speed they were unable to deliver.

Another one, on a porch.

It walked down the stairs.

Shimmers.

Not quite shadows.

Trying to see all of them at once forced him to slow down before he collided with a tree; his left hand waved at them, shooing them weakly. At the intersection he crossed over without looking, and a car had to swerve around him, horn screaming, driver cursing, and he stumbled after it for several steps, lips moving in an apology and unable to find the words.

By a mailbox, a small one.

Standing.

The light rain rolling off it, almost but not quite giving it a face.

He stubbed his toe on the curb, nearly fell, ran a few paces before slowing to a limp, a hand tight against his stomach. Blood hissed in his ears as the rain hissed and tires hissed and his breath hissed between his teeth.

He was supposed to be somewhere.

Blinking away the raindrops didn't help. Wiping a hand across his matted hair didn't help. Moaning aloud didn't help.

One sat on a tire swing—it didn't have a face, and the swing didn't move.

Where was he supposed to be?

The guy in the bar—what the hell was his name?—he might help, but Kayman didn't know where he lived; and even if he did, he wasn't sure he could find it. The houses all looked alike, all of them old, all of them darkening as the shower increased, all of them without light as the afternoon lost its sun, all of them sitting back there like animals waiting in the high grass for something to come along to feed them for the night.

Behind him there were four, walking hand in hand, the rain drawing them, clothing still too blurry to have lines.

One stood in the middle of the street.

When he turned away, one stood not three feet away.

He screamed softly and ran.

It had no face, but he had seen lips moving.

He could see right through it, but it wasn't a ghost.

He slid sharply on a wet leaf, right leg jerking out, something pulling in his groin as he skipped to catch up and keep from falling. He whimpered. His shirt molded itself to his chest and back, pulling him down at the shoulders, running water over his pants that added a hundred pounds to the weight he carried. Water sloshed in his shoes.

He ran.

As best he could, he ran.

Help me, Estelle, Jesus God, help me.

Ran.

Shapes and shadows and indistinct outlines walked on.

Estelle?

Electricity traveled along a wire inside his arm, sped across the top of his chest, and vanished somewhere in the vicinity of his heart.

He cried out.

And ran on.

You're killing yourself, Kayman, Jesus, you're killing yourself.

A boy in a baseball cap rode past him on a bike, whistling.

The thump of windshield wipers on a car idling at the corner before pulling away.

He smiled and showed his teeth. He had liked the rain at one time in his life, liked to walk in it, get wet with it, take a good long hot shower after it and cuddle with Estelle on the couch and listen to it beat helplessly against the roof, glide in trails and ladders down the panes, fill the gutters and roll the acorns away.

One stood in a puddle near a storm drain.

Faceless.

Darker, indefinite form filling in drop by drop.

Another line of electric fire finally slowed him down while he searched the rain for someone he knew, someplace he knew, arms hanging at his sides. Shambling zigzag across the sidewalk, unable anymore to pick his feet up.

Car horns.

A pickup swinging around a corner as he reached it, splashing him, the passenger in the cab waving a quick *hey, we're sorry, old man* before it vanished into the rain.

Into the twilight that arrived several hours too soon.

He nearly fell off the curb, nearly tripped up the other side, staring straight ahead, mouth open, water dripping from his lower lip, his eyebrows, his earlobes, the tips of his fingers twitching by his sides.

Electric fire.

I'm going to die.

Falling at last against a slick telephone pole and laying his cheek against the wood, sobbing harshly, swallowing, praying someone would find him and stop, take his hand, lead him home, Jesus God, he was an old man, he didn't deserve to die like this, he wanted to go home, wanted his bed, wanted to go home, Estelle, for god's sake, please come and take me home.

One stood in front of him. Watching.

He tried to wave it away, but he couldn't lift his arm.

Watching.

Without a face.

He tried to ask it who it was, what it was, but there were only stutters and moans and a slow shake of his head that seemed to free him from the pole, and he stumbled on, knees bent, shoulders sagging forward, turning slowly like a poorly hanged figure spinning slowly in the wind, turning until he recognized a lawn ornament just ahead. A brown deer, lying in the grass, facing the street.

"Oh god," he whispered. "Oh god, please let it be."

When he came abreast of it, he stopped, swayed, stared at the familiar Cape Cod with the plaster dwarf beside the porch steps and waited for something to take it away, blow it out of reach, tell him it was only a rain mirage.

It remained.

He grinned.

He pushed at the air with both hands to get him moving again, two more houses down; all he had to do was get two more houses down.

He knew he had made it when he saw Ronnie standing in the middle of the street, untouched by the rain, defined by the rain, hands clasped at her belly, staring straight ahead.

"Go away," he said, wheezing, falling into a fit of coughing that propelled him up the drive to the steps he managed to trip on only once, to the porch where he fell into the nearest chair and closed his eyes, hands over his face, smelling the rain and his sweat and the sour stench of his fear.

Not stirring when the screen door opened, or when he heard footsteps on the floor.

"Where the hell have you been?"

He couldn't answer Norma, and didn't want to. He was home. He was safe. Nothing could touch him now.

"Damn, are you okay?"

The cold made him rigid save for the movement of his palms over his face, up and down, only an inch either way, up and down, drying himself off, hiding the rain shadows, hiding Ronnie.

"Jesus."

She went back inside. Voices. Footsteps. The screen

door—goddamn, he'd fix that damn thing first thing in the damn morning—and a dry towel being worked over his hair.

"I was scared," Estelle said, though her hands were firm. "I didn't know where you'd gone."

He mumbled something into his hands.

"We tried everywhere, even the Ring, but you weren't there."

His legs began to shake, and he couldn't control them.

"Norma said you'd just gone for a walk, we could wait for you here."

Hair pulled; she wasn't happy. He winced and lowered his hands, gripped the armrests tightly, and when his head was yanked back, looked into her eyes. They were red, puffy; she'd been crying.

"I'm sorry," he said. "I didn't mean ... I'm sorry."

She dropped a second towel into his lap, and he used it to dry his hands and wipe ineffectually at his shirt.

"She's dead," Norma said, and fresh tears wet her cheeks.

"Huh?"

She tossed the towel away and grabbed a handful of hair. "Damn you, she's *dead!* And where the hell were you?" She snapped his head back, forward, back again, until he grabbed her wrists, but he couldn't stop her.

"Dead!"

His head hit the wall.

"Dead! Where the hell were you?"

His head hit the wall.

He couldn't stop her.

"Bastard, where the hell were you?"

He couldn't stop her, he couldn't talk, he couldn't bring himself to try to hit her, so his head struck the wall again and there were lights that danced in the falling rain, music that fell with the water from the eaves, electric fire in his wrists and chest until Norma pulled her away and held her close, rubbing her back, almost rocking her in place.

"What . . . ?" Kayman closed his eyes, but the lights were only worse.

"That doctor friend of yours, Sholcroft?"

He nodded, and winced, and couldn't move his arms.

"Not an hour ago, they found her car out on Chancellor, near the college."

Oh god, he thought, and felt his own tears.

"A boulder."

Oh Jesus.

Estelle broke away from Norma's embrace and ran into the house, wailing, cursing him, cursing God, incongruously cursing each of her children by name.

Norma wouldn't meet his gaze; he was surprised to see she was embarrassed. "She wanted you here. Estelle, that is. The cops called because your name was on that emergency card in her wallet."

"Oh Jesus."

"Instant, they said."

It's never instant, he wanted to tell her. It doesn't make any difference how it is, it's never instant.

"You okay?" Gruff again, protecting Estelle.

He dared not nod, could not shrug.

"So where the hell were you?" she asked quietly, without accusation.

"Lost," was what he said when he could finally speak without sobbing.

She didn't respond.

He didn't explain.

The rain in pale drops from the gutters.

"You better get out of those clothes, Kayman. Estelle doesn't need you sick on top of everything else."

His fault, he thought; he had driven her away with his madness, and she had driven into a rock. And now Estelle, terrified and needing him, and he hadn't been there either, too busy fleeing from demons that didn't exist for anyone but him.

He leaned forward and stared blindly at the street, at the storm.

When finally he stood, Norma was gone. No matter. It was Estelle he had to see, talk to, explain things to.

The door made no sound when he opened it and went inside, the stairs didn't creak when he climbed them and hurried down the hall to their bedroom. "Better change," he said as he walked in. "Gonna catch my d— pneumonia, if I'm not careful." He walked straight to his closet and reached in for a clean shirt, his free hand lightly rubbing his chest, and freezing him when he realized the shirt he wore was dry. "Well," he said, looking over his shoulder, "guess I was out there longer than—"

She was gone.

"Estelle?"

Not anywhere in the room, or the bathroom, the spare room never used once her children had stopped their visits a hundred years ago.

"Estelle?"

Not in the living room, the dining room, the kitchen, the basement. Not her, not her smell, not a sound of her moving ahead of him, keeping just out of sight.

"Estelle?"

She wasn't on the porch.

Norma was gone as well, and he figured the two of them

must have gone to the teacher's house, nothing to worry about. Estelle was upset—angered and grieving and without the comfort he should have given her. It was all right. He'd just walk over there and hold her and sooner or later the rain would end and it would all be all right.

He stepped outside, grinned at himself for forgetting an umbrella, he didn't need to be drenched a second time that day, and turned to open the door.

Flory stood on the top step.

Electric fire.

"Come with me, Kayman," she said, smiling, wearing the same blouse and jacket she had worn when they'd spoken.

He gasped.

The smile wavered, lost its humor.

"Kayman, come with me, please."

He ran, pushing himself through the house and out the back door, wincing at the rain stinging, then pounding, his head, swinging around the corner and down the driveway, running and not moving much faster than a brisk old man's walk. Across the street, feet casting waves in large puddles, and up to the next corner where he turned into the next block and slowed, looked over his shoulder, saw nothing but the rain that turned the air grey.

Norma's door was unlocked; no one was there.

Flory stood on the sidewalk: "Kayman, come with me."

He tried other doors along the street, warm lights in the windows, at the foot of drives, over garages; no one was home.

"Kayman," Flory said.

No car to flee in; he used his legs instead, forcing himself to ignore the fire—the electric pain, that stitched a scar across his middle—reaching Centre Street without realizing it until he found himself panting in front of the police station. Drowned rat, he thought as he hastened inside; god, I must look like a drowned rat.

No one was there.

He called; he yelled; he slammed through the gate in the low wood railing and slammed open all the doors of all the offices he could find.

No one was there.

Flory stood in the rain: "Kayman, come with me."

He could barely move, barely breathe through his mouth while his lips felt bound in ice. He nearly fell down the steps slick with water, fell against a car parked at the curb, swallowed, didn't move when something cool passed over his shoulder and she beckoned him again.

His eyes closed. Suddenly he felt so old, so frightfully, terrifyingly old that "Where?" was little more than a deathbed whisper.

She said nothing, and in the silence of the rain he looked up and over the automobile's roof. Johnny stood on the sidewalk across the street, Brenda beside him. They waved and walked away, west toward Mainland Road. Before they reached the corner, the rain had erased them, but he could still see the smoke from Johnny's cigarette floating for a while before the rain erased that too.

"Is it over?" he asked. "Am I . . . is it over?"

Fighting, rebelling, denying, praying that the downhill slope wouldn't be quite so steep, quite so rocky that the slide would be more gentle. More right.

"Come with me, Kayman."

Streetlights and house lights and the splash of rain; cold and a cold wind, cold skin, in a twilight that hid the sky but not the town around him; too weary to think, to find reason, to find something in his madness that would give him a clue so he could find his way back, to the house and Estelle and what the hell did it matter, Jesus God, he was tired. So goddamn tired. Everything about him, inside and out, ached, begged him to find a bed, demanded he stop moving.

And then a flash of anger that they had left him after all.

An old man alone.

Walking in the rain with a ghost that only proved how mad he really was.

"You know," he said, and Flory's head tilted; she was listening. His left hand flapped at his side. "I guess it really is like Ronnie said once—god, that was a long time ago—that the best you can do is hold on. There's no stardom, no wealth, not much of anything but just holding on for people like me. Maybe you, too, I don't know." The hand stopped; the other one started. "I make furniture, you know. Pretty good stuff, too. It . . ." He squinted into the rain, no longer feeling it, no longer caring. "It just wasn't good enough. It didn't look like anything else, you know? It made itself sometimes, and it wasn't . . ."

At Mainland Road he saw the fence of Pilgrim's Travelers.

He stopped.

"You know that song, all those books, about doing it your way, the hell with what people think?"

"Come with me, Kayman," she said, crossing over.

He glanced behind him, looked ahead, watched her glide through falling water.

"When you get old," he said quietly, "and you don't have to be very old, hell, you could be fifty, I was pretty close to it, it's a goddamn son of a bitching thing," he shouted, "when you got to start the hell all over again!" He crossed the road, a fist swiping at the rain. "You know that? You know it?" His voice lowered. "No. You don't know that. You don't know that at all."

She stood under the arch, waiting.

"What the hell do you want?" he demanded, looking around her to the deserted midway. "It's closed."

She waited.

In the rain.

"Where is Estelle?" There were no colors left that he could see; it felt like a graveyard. "Flory, where did everybody go?"

She held out her hand.

He didn't take it. He had never touched Johnny or Brenda, not even Ronnie though there were times when he wanted to strangle her, or punch her, or give her a good swift kick. No touching. That was some kind of rule.

She held out her hand.

If I go in there, he thought, I'm never coming out.

"No," he said firmly. "It ain't gonna rain forever."

Water dripped from the tips of her fingers.

"Just tell me what the hell's going on."

And hating the sound of pleading in his voice, he took the hand after all, and it was cold; he followed her in, and it was cold; yet he didn't think he was dead, because he could feel the muddy ground, slipped on it a couple of times, once leaned down and brushed a hand over it and it felt gritty and touched with slime.

The concessions were boarded up, pennants sagging, droplets of water racing along the guy wires, streamers of mist beginning to lift off the mud. He watched them, fascinated, remembered with a half-smile how he had done the same when he was a kid, watching the ragged plumes of white rise from the street whenever there was a shower, defiant of the weather that had created them, sometimes merging into small clouds the wind quickly carried into the trees or hedges or into the sky, where they were lost.

"If you're a ghost," he said, "why can I feel you?"

He squeezed her hand.

It squeezed back.

"Flory, come on, you've got to tell me . . ."

They stepped into the oval, and he saw the black carousel.

He tried to stop; she pulled him on.

He grabbed her hand with both of his and tried to break her grip; she pulled him on.

"No," was all he could do; all his strength was gone.

"Please," was all he could do; the mist-feathers rose and took form, the white sliding away from figures and shadows and shapes that began to move toward the carousel as well; "Please," was all he whispered.

But none climbed aboard.

"Flory."

"Merry-go-round," she said, turning to him with that smile. "Get on, Kayman, or I'll kill you."

Too shocked to argue, he used a stained brass pole to pull himself up, and leaned against it.

Shapes.

Shadows.

Not one of them had a face.

"Ride," she said.

The carousel shuddered.

Then Ronnie was there, somewhere in the back; Johnny leaning against the iron rail, his arm around Brenda's shoulder.

"I'm not dead," he said.

"Oh no," Flory answered. "That would be too easy."

Directly behind him a Bengal tiger. Kayman's legs were stiff, his hands cramped, but he found a way into the saddle, and gripped the pole with both hands. Afraid to fall. Afraid to move.

Music tin and silver.

The tiger moved, the lights moved, so slowly it was easy for Flory to walk along, keeping pace.

"If I'm not dead," he said, "then they are?" A nod to the shapes, the shadows, created by the rain. He included her without meaning to, and the realization, the remembering, made him moan.

But she said, "No, Kayman. Not all of them."

A little faster.

She fell slightly behind.

Of course not, he thought, as if it were the most logical thing in the world, Johnny hadn't died; he had wanted to move to New York where, he'd claimed, his writing would be better appreciated. They had fought. Not argued or debated. They'd shouted, punched the air, danced around each other the way they'd done when they were kids and in the throes of unreasoning temper. He had left before—the army, traveling, a short-lived job in Texas, but he had always returned. This, however, had been different; this had been an *I'll come back to visit when I can*, at a time when Kayman had been alone, left alone, struggling with reasons why, screaming at God, feeling the press of years that gave him increasingly less room to maneuver in, hide in, regroup and rebuild and start again in.

An empty time.

Flory took hold of a post as the carousel picked up speed, and swung herself lightly to the platform.

He should have been afraid. She was dead after all, and she stood beside him. He should have been afraid, and he was— but not of that.

Because she had left him, and she was still here.

The music.

The glittering mirrors spinning in the opposite direction.

He watched the rain sheet off the roof, watched the shapes and shadows, caught a glimpse of Brenda dancing with Johnny.

Saw Ronnie beside the ticket booth.

She was smiling.

The next time around she waved to him, and his hand automatically began to respond until he realized what he was doing, yanked it into his lap and noticed a shape behind her, in the rain, and he frowned because, faceless, it was nevertheless familiar.

"You don't remember," Flory said.

"No. But—"

"You forgot him."

She reached over and touched his leg, patted it, stroked it once, and said, "Let them go, Kayman. Let us go," before jumping off, running to keep from falling, then, as he looked over his shoulder so as not to lose sight of her, standing there.

Standing when he came around again, hands at her sides.

In the rain filled with ghosts he could no longer remember.

As easy as that, then: let them go and the carousel would release him. He couldn't just jump off. He was too old. He would fall. Break a bone. Break a hip, perhaps, which would eventually kill him. Just let them go.

Let them leave.

And then what, he asked the shapes and Johnny and the shadows and Brenda and the almost familiar and smiling, waving Ronnie; what will happen then?

He stared straight ahead, trying to think, not marking the hours, not seeing the dark until the dark was nearly done.

What would happen?

Nothing.

The carousel would slow down, the music would stop, the

lights would switch off one by one, and there would always be Estelle, always, and the ill-tempered Norma Hobbs, and May-ard Chase to help him find a way with his carpentry, and the people he drank with at the Ring and the Crow, and the town itself marking him one of them.

Nothing would happen.

Except, that night, they had all joined the rain.

Estelle stood by Johnny the next time he saw him.

Norma whispered to Ronnie when he saw the ticket booth again.

Let them go.

Let the carousel stop and the music stop and the lights switch off, and go home. And the next time it rained they would be with him on the porch, Johnny teasing Brenda, Ronnie telling him what it was like to be not dead, Estelle rocking with him, forever safe from her children.

The music began to die.

I don't know, he thought; I don't know.

The carousel began to slow.

I just don't know.

Let them go and they vanish, the dead to wherever the dead need to rest, the others perhaps to living, perhaps to join the ghosts.

Either way, in the rain, in the sun, he'd be alone.

The music stopped when the carousel did.

And in the last hour of the dead, he sat on the tiger and watched the rain end.

Nothing left now but mud and cloud and the flapping of a pennant like the snap of a listless whip.

All he had to say was *yes*.

But he didn't know.

Oh god, he didn't know.

EPILOGUE

THE MUSIC SUBSIDED WHEN SOMEONE TURNED THE volume down, the voices drifted softer, the sounds of frantic movement gone. The parade of bicycles on the street had stopped long ago. From the backyard there was laughter, but easier, not as forced. Cyd Yarrow came out with a tray in one hand, asking for empty glasses, empty plates, littering would be punished by having to listen to heavy metal without benefit of parole; we obliged instantly, with laughing thanks, and when we were alone again tried to get a fix on the time without looking at our watches, without looking at one another. But time very often means little around here, and no one offered to judge who was right, who was wrong.

Finally Deric scratched the back of one ear and looked at me with no expression and asking questions just the same.

I didn't answer.

Wes Martin had taken over the police chief's role when Abe Stockton had ... died is as good a word as any, I suppose, though I'm the only one who didn't use it; then, not long after, poor Wes had dropped dead of a heart attack trying to unravel a traffic snarl in the middle of Chancellor Avenue. He was barely into his late forties. Though no one said anything publicly, it was clear from the swift decision of the town council to contact Deric that someone believed that only a Stockton could hold the job.

I didn't answer that one either.

It wasn't my place to force or nurture belief. I simply told the stories. What he did with them, what anyone did who had ever sat with me and listened, wasn't my concern. Dismissed as clumsy fables, passed over as bonfire tales, accepted literally or scoffed at—in the long run it didn't matter except to those whose lives I told.

Nina lit a cigarette with a flourish I feared would burn my house down.

Callum suggested we go inside and join the others in case they thought we were engaged in something illegal and disgusting out here on the steps.

And I watched Deric, charted his confusion, saw behind his eyes him marking what I had said beside what his brother had told him over the years. Deric had never been to Oxrun Station; his only contact with us had been his brother. Perhaps, as the infrequent letters had arrived, he had decided they were the hints and musings of an old man trying to make something of his past, creating a little excitement for a small and unexciting town so it would have all been worthwhile; perhaps, as the infrequent letters had arrived, he had feared for his brother's mind as it neared eight decades of living and began to lose track; and perhaps, while in bed and listening to the dark around him, he believed every word.

I think he wanted to.

I think he was afraid to.

Which is what made me stand and stretch suddenly and loudly, startling Callum, bringing Nina quickly to her feet and looking around as if searching for some monster crouching in the porch shadows.

"Walk," I said, smiling the way I imagined a shark did when he saw an innocent, stupid minnow. "I think it's time for a brisk walk before I get too stiff to move and have to sleep out here tonight." I started across the lawn. "You can come if you want. It wouldn't kill you, you know."

"What about the party?" Callum asked.

"It isn't my party."

"It's your house."

"So? Deric's the honored guest and he's out here with us."

I paused on the sidewalk and took a slow deep breath, summer air just a comfortable step away from cool. Deric was with me before I'd gone a dozen paces, Nina a few more, Callum grumbling behind about all the food he had missed because he had to humor the nut. I winked at him. He sneered back and wanted to know if Nina feared for her virtue, strolling as she was in the middle of the night with three obviously unrepentant reprobates out to raise a little hell.

"One's a cop," she reminded him, grinning at Deric.

Stockton grinned back.

"Swell," Callum muttered. "The record lady's a smartass." He dodged her kick, reached out, and poked my shoulder. "So where are we going?"

"Around."

He knew me better. "Around where."

"Armstrong's farm."

"Damn. I figured."

"What's the matter?" Deric said.

Callum grabbed up a twig, snapped it, threw it into the street. "Nothing," he said, "that a comet landing on my head wouldn't cure."

Once on Chancellor Avenue we headed west, alone on the street, most of the houses dark, leaves talking to themselves over our heads. Footsteps not quite loud, and too loud; words begun, and not completed; hands fluttering and flapping into and out of pockets, into and out of clasps, scratching, smoothing, rubbing, pointing out the well-lighted Chancellor Inn, the direction of the hospital, trying to inscribe a permanent map in the air to show the Station's relationship to Massachusetts and New York.

I had a feeling we looked pretty damn drunk, and I laughed to myself.

Then Deric said, "What's Armstrong's farm?"

"It's deserted," Nina told him before I could answer. "On the other side of the highway. Some guy who used to live there a zillion years ago. Nobody knows why he left. There isn't much left of it now—weeds, stickers, an apple orchard nobody will touch with a ten-foot pole, some fields mostly covered with new forest growth now." She shrugged. "Not the most exciting place in the world."

"So why are we going there?"

"Don't ask me, ask him," she said. "He's the guide."

I put a finger to my lips.

She slapped my arm. "Tell him, dope, before he runs away."

I shook my head.

Deric's patience was amazing.

At Mainland Road we paused for a moment, not waiting for traffic, just standing there a while so our vision could adjust to the glow from the sky. Across the way, the ditch was darker black, the high shrubs and thorn bushes more like a stone wall.

"I ain't going to fly," Callum grumbled as we crossed.

"There are ways," I told him, and found a gap and led them through.

And once on the other side, Deric stopped me with a touch.

"Pilgrim's Travelers was here?"

I nodded.

"I see."

I knew what he was thinking—though moonlight and starlight weren't their brightest tonight, it was more than clear, and would have been so in pitch black, that nothing the size of that itinerant carnival could have fit into the open space between the thorns and the orchard, and the trees that flanked them. Not even half. Not even a quarter.

There simply wasn't any room.

And there were too many rocks, too many boulders, too many saplings and yearlings and old weeds and depressions and burrows and wildflowers. This place hadn't been used since King George was in charge.

Nina stood close, fumbled for my hand and held it; hers was cool.

Callum followed Deric here and there, answering questions I couldn't hear, staring at the ground, hunkering down and poking at the earth with a stick or a finger, standing, looking up, finally turning to me and waiting with his hands loose on his hips, looking every inch a cop demanding explanations.

There wasn't much more I could tell him.

Casey Bethune went on vacation and hasn't been seen since, his house looking as if it hadn't been lived in for years;

on the other hand, his famed gardens had grown wild in that time, and despite the neglect were amazingly lovely after each summer rain. Especially the roses.

There was speculation among the regulars at the Brass Ring that he'd run off with Norma Hobbs. Few believed it. Tina Elby claimed her friend had been murdered. Few believed that either. Norma, they claimed, was just too damn mean to die. Closer to the truth was the notion that she, at Kayman Kalb's behest, had taken Estelle someplace west where Estelle's children couldn't find her. They'd been back a couple of times—a more obnoxious pair I'd never met—threatening lawsuits and arrest and a government investigation, but old Kayman didn't seem to care. He just sat on his porch no matter what the weather was. Rocking. Watching the street. Every so often walking over to the Ring or up to the Crow and having a drink. Always alone.

He talks to himself a lot.

Nobody minds; he's one of ours.

Sadly, the Lumbairds were forced to move back to Cambridge when Neal lost his already tenuous job.

Rene Saxton, shortly after the mass funeral for her sister and family, took over the insurance office in Harley and was, by all accounts, practically minting her own money. Her son did well at Hawksted College and still worked on occasion at the *Station Herald*. He was, as they used to say, a good boy, who loved his mother.

"So . . ." Stockton said thoughtfully, a hand turning me around and starting us back.

I nodded. "They're holding on, Deric. They're holding on."

In the middle of the highway Nina stopped, grabbed my arm, and pointed up and west. "Hey!"

We looked.

"Make a wish," she said quietly.

A shooting star, flaring green in an arc that took it behind the deserted farm.

She pinched me lightly. "So, smarty, where did it land, where can we find it?"

It didn't, and we can't.

It flares, and there is no grave.

"Well, that's all well and good," Callum said, holding his watch close to his eyes, "but I'm bloody damn thirsty, and if we hurry, we can still make last call at the Inn."

Nina agreed, urged us on, but Deric and I stopped when we reached the other side.

I wasn't going to, though; I was hoping he hadn't heard.

But he had.

It was obvious in the way his face took on a mask of the melancholy that comes only deep into morning, after midnight and before the sun.

He looked at me; he looked back at the field; he shook his head; he walked on.

I joined him a step behind as the night breeze pushed me gently, and my shadow merged with his, and we both ignored the carousel.

Playing music.

Tin and silver.

Slipping away like the shooting star.

Leaving us here.

Holding on.